VENOMOUS

A SAVING ABBIE NOVELLA

MAGGIE ALABASTER

So Good
   Written by Abbie Hart

My love was a dark place,
   Betrayed, denied, and broken.
   I was shattered,
   Over and gone.
   Over and gone.
   So gone.

One night I saw you,
   And everything changed.
   You put your arms 'round my world,
   Broke all the chains.
   All of the chains.
   The chains.

Nothing can hold me back,
   When you're holding me.
   So many become one,
   So hard, yet so easy.
   So fucking easy.
   So easy.

You have my whole heart,
   Soul and body too.
   Forever, I'll have,

Every one of you.
So fucking easy.
So fucking good.
So good.
So incredibly good.

ABBIE

"I thought you said we were arriving in style." Penn looked over the back of his seat at Jackson, his eyes narrowed. "If this tin can rocks any harder, I'm going to puke on your shoes."

"This tin can," Jackson said slowly, "is worth a year's worth of wages. Yours, not mine. For the record, a small commercial aircraft would have bounced much worse than this one. If you prefer, I'll organise a boat to take you back to mainland North America?"

Penn made a rude sound in the back of his throat and turned away.

I put a hand on Jackson's thigh and squeezed, but my eyes were on the back of Penn's head.

"I think you should organise a *rowboat* for Penn." I

couldn't resist teasing the keyboardist. He'd do the same to me if I was the one feeling sick.

Without looking back at me, Penn raised his hand and flipped me off. "It's not my fault if I get travel sick on small craft."

"No, but it's your fault we have to hear about it," Asher said from across the aisle. "Jackson finally organised a private jet for us and you're still not happy."

"I think it's awesome." I leaned my head against Jackson's shoulder and smiled up at him.

"I'm glad someone thinks so." Jackson lightly kissed my forehead. As manager of Wolf Venom, the hottest rock band in the world right now, and me, the slightly less popular soloist, he had enough on his plate without Penn complaining about everything.

Sometimes I wondered if Penn wasn't happy unless he had something to complain about. I loved the band's keyboardist as much as I loved the other six guys, but sometimes he could be a pain in every-one's ass.

"I think it's awesome too," Asher said. The band's drummer was an easy-going jokester, who usually put a positive spin on things, even the worst situation. His inappropriate humour at the wrong moment almost got us killed a couple of times in the past, but we got through. We always did.

"I agree." Zeke Brantley was the band's lead singer and unofficial leader in times of danger. When we came under attack by gangsters who were after him and his mobster family, he was the one we followed. If not for him, we'd all be dead right now. Especially him.

Good times.

He was also Asher's boyfriend as well as mine. "I think the label should spring for a private jet more often. Although, maybe with a king-sized bed next time." He grinned as Jackson turned to frown at him.

"Rowboat for two," Jackson said wryly. "Maybe you and Penn could race the plane back to Florida."

We all laughed, except Penn, who turned around to give him a dirty look.

"Don't encourage Zeke," he said. "That's exactly the kind of challenge he'd take."

Channing, the band's saxophonist, twisted around in his seat. "Are you afraid you'll lose?" he taunted.

"Rowboat versus a plane, what do you fucking think?" Penn retorted. "But you reminded me, it's past time we had that rematch. You, me, sandy beach. Let's see who can run fastest then. It'll still be me." He beat Channing back in Munich, weeks ago, but that was on paved ground. Sand would be a lot harder, given that it's a lot... you know, softer.

"You're on," Channing said. "I look forward to kicking your butt this time. Maybe we should make it interesting."

"You don't think this whole tour was interesting?" Landon asked. The rhythm guitarist's eyes were wide.

"He has a point," Tully said. The lead guitarist sat alone in front of Zeke and Asher, stretched out across two seats. "We almost died a time or two."

"Don't remind us," Jackson said. "Let's just enjoy IslandFest and put all of that behind us."

"Good idea," I said. "But I'm curious what Channing has in mind for a bet." Neither of them needed money, but they were so competitive, bragging rights wouldn't be enough.

"I'll think of something," Channing said.

"I can see the island," Asher said, drawing everyone's attention to him. He pointed excitedly at the window, his face pressed against it like he was a five-year-old boy, not a man in his mid-twenties. Whatever, we'd all agreed growing up was probably overrated anyway.

I looked out the window beside me at the sparkling ocean. It was dotted with boats, most heading in the same direction. IslandFest was going to be enormous.

Five days of rock music, partying and more music. Two hundred thousand concert goers would descend on the island. A hundred and fifty of the best bands in the world, and who knows how many up-and-coming artists, ready to perform in different locations around the island.

It was going to be incredible. I could hardly believe I was a part of it. Me, Abbie Hart. This was dream come true stuff right here. I wouldn't pinch myself in case I woke.

Without warning, the plane dropped a few metres. I made a face and swallowed hard to hold down my breakfast.

Penn groaned and his head disappeared. I peered between the seats to see him bent double, head between his knees.

"Are you—" I groaned as the plane dropped again. "That rowboat is sounding better and better."

"Sorry folks," the voice of the pilot came over the speakers. "An offshore breeze is creating turbulence. We'll be landing in about ten minutes, so buckle up."

We all hurried to do as he suggested, right at the same moment the plane dropped for a third time before rising again.

Penn popped back up long enough to say, "Was this plane made by one of your asshole families? It seems to hate me as much as they do." He disappeared again.

I smiled. He liked to pretend he was an asshole, and he wouldn't agree if he heard me say this, but he was sweet at times. All of the guys were. Besides, he had a point about the plane. Or at least, the turbulence. I didn't think even mobsters could control the weather. Yet.

"Maybe that offshore breeze is Penn's farts," Asher said. "He might be causing it."

Muffled words came from Penn's direction that sounded a lot like, "Fuck off," followed by, "It's probably bad air from Asher's ass."

"At least they haven't lost their sense of humour," I said to Jackson.

He laughed softly. "I've never known them to lose that. Other things, yes, but never that." He and I only became close in the last couple of weeks and we were still trying to sort out where he fit in with the rest of my boyfriends. He was their manager and their friend but he was also their family, with or without me.

It was…awkward, but we'd figure it out. Hopefully IslandFest would give us the chance we needed to do so. Including finding time to be alone, just the two of us. We looked for opportunities for the last couple of weeks but none had arisen, so to speak. With the world tour coming to an end, we were all busy and exhausted. A couple of days on the island before the festival started might be just what we all needed.

Sun, surf and sand, cocktails and my guys. Sounded like heaven to me. After this, we'd be off home, back to Australia. Back to our normal lives. The new normal that was, in which I was dating seven guys. Yeah, mind blowing isn't it?

"I can see the runway," Asher said. He looked around and frowned. "I just realised something."

His expression made my heart race. What the hell was wrong now? Hadn't we been through enough?

Evidently I wasn't the only one thinking exactly that. Everyone turned to look at him with more or less the same expression on their face. Worried with an air of freaked the fuck out.

"What did you realise, babe?" Zeke asked. His gorgeous face was creased in concern, laced with barely contained violence. He always seemed on the verge of punching the shit out of someone, or blowing their brains out.

"I realised," Asher said slowly, "that we should have parachuted down. Think of the entrance we would have made." He threw his hands up and raised his eyes like he was watching us fall from the sky towards him. A smile tugged on the corners of his mouth.

Penn sat up. "Who votes we throw Asher out right now?" He raised his hand. "We could open the festival with a splat instead of a bang."

"I know you love me," Asher told him. "That's why you wouldn't do that."

"I wouldn't do it because it would put the rest of us in danger," Penn said. "Otherwise, I'd totally do it. I bet Tully would help me."

Tully raised both of his hands, palms forward. "Leave me out of it, dude. I'm not throwing anyone out of a plane unless they're trying to kill one of us. If they are, then all bets are off. And so are they."

I believed him. If he had to, he'd kill to protect us. And he had. Most of us had. I didn't want to dwell on that anymore. The nightmares were enough.

"No one on this plane is trying to kill anyone else on this plane," Jackson said firmly. "Including the pilot, who is an old friend of Levi's."

The owner of our label, White Wolf Records, certainly knew some interesting people. But then, if anyone was going to know someone with a private jet, it would be Levi Jones. To say he was connected was an understatement. He also gave me a chance when I needed it more than anything. He signed me after my former label terminated my contract and no one else would touch me. Without him I wouldn't have my career or any of my guys.

"That's good to know," I said. "I'm almost certain the turbulence is a natural occurrence." After everything I'd seen and done in the last few months, I wouldn't rule out anything anymore. Even something as crazy as that.

He curled his fingers around mine. "It's one of those things, that's all. We'll be fine. I promise. Nothing bad is going to happen to you. It can't, because I have plans for us." His deep, rumbly tone left me in no doubt what he meant. A jolt of pure fire lanced right down to my core.

I looked up into his denim blue eyes. "You do? What is it?"

His eyebrows twitched and he smiled. He was clueless how hot he was. That was part of his charm.

"I'm not telling you. If I did, that would ruin the surprise. Trust me, you're going to love it."

"I do trust you," I said. "I'm sure whatever it is, it will be amazing." My heart stuttered at the thought of being alone with him. With six other boyfriends, I had no shortage of orgasms, but that didn't make me want him any less. If anything, waiting so long for this made me want him more. Semi-forbidden fruit and all that.

The lines around his eyes crinkled slightly as he

frowned. "Now I'm worried I oversold it a little bit. Should I have just said you'll like it?" His eyes shone with humour.

"Always start low," Zeke said. "Then no one has high expectations."

"Are you speaking from experience?" Asher asked. "Because you always start with a high bar."

"That's because I know I can meet those expectations," Zeke said smugly.

"Thanks," Jackson said sarcastically. "You think I can't? You have that little faith in my organisational skills?" He made a face but clearly wasn't offended. We all knew his organisational skills were second to none. That was one of the reasons he was such a good manager. One of many reasons.

Zeke grinned. "Of course not. On the other hand, if you do something amazing, that's going to make it harder for the rest of us to impress Abbie." He looked totally unconcerned that might be an actual problem.

"I don't need to try to impress her," Penn said. "She's seen my cock. She's already impressed."

I couldn't argue with that. His cock *was* impressive. They all were, just like the guys they were attached to.

"If she's impressed by your cock, then the bar is really low," Asher teased.

"At least she can see mine," Penn said. "Unlike yours, mine is bigger than a pencil."

Asher laughed. "I've never seen a pencil as big as my dick. How would you write with it? It would be too long and thick."

"Long and thick, sounds like an accurate description of your head," Penn said.

"It sounds like an accurate description of both of your heads," Channing teased. He lightened up in the last few weeks, and joined in the teasing more often.

I shook my head at them all. They wouldn't be them if they didn't give each other hell. At the end of the day, all of the guys were closer than brothers. Their bond with me and with each other was unbreakable. Even when the situation was difficult, or deadly, we pulled through together.

We could survive a week of drinking, partying and music on a tropical island in the Caribbean.

I mean, what could go wrong? Right?

Okay, plenty.

2

ABBIE

"This is amazing." Landon's eyes were huge as he looked around one of the rooms. We had two, with a door between them, and a bathroom for each room. The door would stay open and we'd gather in one room, like we usually did. Not many hotels accommodated polyamorous groups of eight. Yet. Give the world some time.

"Yeah, it's not bad," Channing agreed. He dragged his suitcase to the corner and left it beside Landon's. Give it five minutes, there would be clothes strewn around everywhere.

"How to say you've been in a lot of five-star hotels without saying you've been in a lot of five-star hotels," Asher teased. He left his suitcase in another corner, with Zeke's and mine. "I think it's amazing."

"It really is," I agreed. The resort was one of many

on the island, and not even the biggest or fanciest, but the view of the ocean a couple of metres from the front steps of the villa was incredible.

"I'm not that easily impressed by places." Channing shrugged. "As long as you two are here, I have all I need."

"Thank you," Zeke said as if Channing was talking about him.

"He means me," Penn said, dragging his suitcase into the other bedroom.

"He means all of us," Asher said. He draped an arm over Channing's shoulder. "Right?"

"Sure." Channing gave him the side eye. "If that's what you want to believe."

Asher patted his back. "It totally is." He lowered his arm and stepped away. "Who's up for a swim?"

"Not you," Jackson said. "You all have an interview in half an hour."

We all turned and gave him a look, including me.

He raised his hands. "What can I say? Have you forgotten you're not here for a holiday?"

"Forgotten, no," Asher said. "In denial, yes. Surprised you couldn't give us a few hours to unwind? Not really."

"Trying to keep your careers on track? Definitely," Jackson retorted. "It shouldn't take long, then you can do whatever you want for the rest of the day.

Within reason," he added quickly. "Don't forget I'm the designated killjoy around here."

I hooked my arm through his. "No you're not. You're just doing what's best for us, because you care."

"And because he gets paid for it," Penn said.

"That too," Jackson agreed. He kissed my nose. "Just so you all know, Abbie and I are going on a date tonight. Try not to burn the resort down while we're gone."

"So much for doing whatever we want for the rest of the night." Asher snaked an arm around my waist and pulled me away from Jackson and to his chest. "I was looking forward to a bunch of fucking." He kissed my mouth, long and slow. His tongue swept across my lips, hungry as always.

Zeke stepped up behind him and wrapped his arms around Asher's neck. "You can still have a bunch of fucking, babe."

"Hell yeah," Asher said. "Although, it's fun when it's three of us. Or more than three."

"I'll pretend there's two or three of me," Zeke said. "By the time I'm done with you, you'll forget there's only one of me."

Asher looked over his shoulder. "I knew there was a reason I loved you. You're epic."

"Fuck yeah, I am," Zeke agreed. "So are you two." He kissed Asher and then me.

"If we keep doing this, we're going to miss that interview," I said. Which was tempting right now, with both guys wrapped around me and each other. The breeze generated by the ceiling fan above me did nothing to cool my blood. With seven guys around me, there was no shortage of stimulation, no lack of fucking either. They always got me going with just a look or a touch anyway. And all of them knew it.

"They won't notice if we're not there." Asher nuzzled his face into my hair.

"They won't notice if *I'm* not there, but they'll notice if you're not," I said firmly.

"They'll notice if *any* of you are missing," Jackson said. "They want to speak to all of you." He gave me a long look when I turned my face to look at him. "You too. I know you haven't had a good relationship with the press in the past, but we're working on changing that. Okay?"

That was the understatement of the year, but I wasn't going to let them get me down anymore. I'd dragged myself up from a black hole with the help of the guys, and the support of my fans. If the press didn't like it, they could get fucked.

Not by me.

Honestly, most of them were nice these days. Of course they were. They caught a sniff of the relationship between me and the guys and wanted to be the ones to break the story. Considering the boost it would give to their careers, they might do almost anything for it.

Good luck with that. We had no plans to discuss it with anyone other than ourselves. As far as we were concerned, it was our business, no one else's. At least until we were ready to make it someone else's business. For now, we'd keep it amongst us.

Although we weren't exactly going out of our way to be discreet. Photos of me with Channing and Landon, and with Asher and Zeke, had all gone viral. Sooner or later, someone would take photos of me with Tully, Penn, Jackson or all of them.

Whatever. If that was all people had to talk about in their day, then maybe they should get themselves a life.

"I know you wouldn't arrange interviews with anyone who would act like a prick," I assured Jackson. "And if they do, that's on them. Not you."

"The label's publicist has been carefully vetting everyone that might want to talk to any of you," Jackson said. "They know if they screw up, they won't get access to you again. Levi is big on giving second chances to people who deserve it, but not those who don't. And he has a *long* memory."

"To match his long bank account balance," Asher said.

"Exactly," Jackson said lightly. He didn't say any more, but we all knew what he was thinking. The guy's bank balances were healthy too. Healthier than his or mine.

When I first met the guys, I was down to my last couple of hundred dollars. I was better off now, but I had a long way to go to catch them. Not that it was a competition. They made it clear on more than one occasion that what was theirs was also mine. Naturally, the opposite was true as well.

On the other hand, I liked to have my own money and not rely on them for anything other than support and orgasms. Lots and lots of orgasms.

I glanced at my phone. "Do I have time to make myself pretty?" I asked.

"You're already pretty, sweetheart," Zeke said immediately.

"It's Asher who needs the help." Penn was leaning against the wall, looking out at the ocean. "But there's not enough time in the day to make him look pretty."

"Fuck off," Asher said cheerfully. "I am pretty. On

the outside and, unlike you, on the inside too." He flashed Penn a sarcastic smile, showing no teeth.

Penn shrugged. "I don't want to be pretty on the inside. That would interfere with my reputation as a badass and an asshole."

"Nothing will interfere with those," Zeke assured him. "You've firmly established yourself as the band asshole."

"Thank you." Penn nodded as though that was an actual compliment. "Don't anyone go forgetting it."

"How could we forget, you keep on reminding us, sir?" I told him. When we first met, we hated each other. Or at least, we gave each other a lot of shit. At the same time, we wanted to fuck each other. Okay, not much changed, but I loved him like crazy. He was an asshole, but he was mine. And loved when I called him sir before I sucked his cock dry.

Penn shrugged and gave me a look so heated it was lucky my panties didn't melt right off .

Whether or not I was pretty was a matter of opinion, but right now I was as wet as hell.

"I might go and fix my make up." By that I meant, change my panties. These guys were all dangerous in the best possible way. They loved driving me wild as much as they liked playing music.

I was one hundred percent here for every moment of it.

Asher gave me a knowing glance of his own and reluctantly unwound his arms from me.

"Okay, but Zeke and I get to take you out for lunch tomorrow. I'd say breakfast, but it sounds like you might be busy with Jackson." He gave us both a lopsided smile. Not one hint of jealousy. If anything, he looked ready to herd everyone out the door so we could be alone.

Tempting, but even if the interviewer didn't notice my absence, they'd notice Jackson's. They'd probably take it as a cue to ask questions they were already told not to ask. At the very least, they'd push their luck as far as they could take it.

That would probably lead to Penn telling them to fuck off. As much as I wanted time alone with Jackson, I didn't want to miss that. Penn was never shy about sharing his feelings, especially when that feeling was irritation, anger or annoyance.

"If I'm lucky," Jackson agreed.

My heart did a triple somersault.

Jackson usually played his cards close to his chest. Today he looked at me like I was the last piece of chocolate, saved just for him. A piece he'd thought about eating for a long time.

Honestly, that was probably accurate. I thought about him eating me for quite some time too. Pretty much since we met. I couldn't wait to see what he had planned. Whatever it was, it would be amazing. Even if it was a simple picnic on the beach, watching the sun set. That sounded perfect to me.

"I won't be long." I stopped to give Jackson a kiss on my way to my suitcase, then pulled out what I needed and stepped into the bathroom.

"Let us know if you need any help," Tully called out after me.

I opened the door and peered back out at him. "You know how to fix makeup?"

He grinned. "No, but I know how to mess it up." Before I could respond he added, "I also know how to avoid messing it up." He winked and wiggled his eyebrows.

I shook my head at him and closed the door again. If we weren't in a hurry, I would take him up on that offer. At this rate, I was going to need shares in a panty factory.

I regarded my reflection in the mirror while I added a little extra mascara and eyeliner, and redid my lipstick.

A few months ago, I would have seen a down and out, desperate singer looking back at me. Now, I looked happy. Happier than I ever had. Never in my wildest dreams could I have imagined living the life I was living right now.

Okay, no one would have imagined the mobster

part, or the seven boyfriends, but if anyone even told me it was possible, I would have told them they were out of their minds. And yet, here I was, in a tropical resort, living my best life.

I was a lucky girl. And very much looking forward to a nice quiet night alone with Jackson.

3

JACKSON

"Oh, wow. Are you kidding me?"

The way her eyes widened, and the smile on her gorgeous mouth, were exactly what I hoped for. What I imagined a hundred times since I thought this up.

"Whose—"

"I borrowed it from the resort manager." I led her over to the back of the vintage motorbike and handed her a helmet. "According to her, it still runs." I knew enough about bikes to know this one was in nearly perfect condition. Perfect for a bike which lived in a place where salt sooner or later attacked everything.

"If it breaks down, we don't have far to walk." I picked up my own helmet and pressed it down onto my head.

We could have walked there to begin with, but how would I impress her if that was how our date started? After all, I was trying to stand out when her other six boyfriends were all famous rock stars. I still wasn't sure what she saw in me—a former bass player turned manager twelve years older than her. I wasn't as buff as the other guys or as cool. I could drive a bus and ride a motorcycle, so there was that. A guy had to use what skills he had.

I had a few more up my sleeve before tonight was done.

She gave me a doubtful look, which I probably deserved, and slipped on her helmet.

I helped her onto the back of the bike and straddled the seat in front of her. "Hold on tight."

My cock was twitchy before she slipped her arms around me. Feeling her pressed hard against my back…

Down boy, I told myself. We had plenty of time for that later.

Who was I kidding? Abbie was absolutely gorgeous and my cock was right to respond to her.

Fortunately, with a couple of days before the festival and being later in the afternoon, the narrow road that circumnavigated the island was almost empty. Apart from a few people walking, and a man riding a bike, we had it to ourselves.

"Do you know we're going?" she said in my ear.

I laughed. The wind dragged the sound away.

"I have some idea," I said over my shoulder. The island wasn't big enough to get lost, and the directions I was given seemed simple enough. Ride past all the resorts until we reached a part of the island that wasn't developed yet. Our destination was right at the end of a spit of land. Everything should be waiting for us.

"This is beautiful," she said as we flew across a small bridge over a stream. On one side was forest, on the other ocean.

"You're beautiful." The view might be jealous of her, but it was a gorgeous part of the world.

"No, you." The breeze swept her laugh away too, but not before it tickled my ear, making me even harder.

"I'm not beautiful." I slowed the bike as we rode onto the spit and headed to the very end. We stopped under a stand of trees and I killed the engine.

"That was amazing." She slipped off the bike and removed her helmet. "I've always wanted to learn to ride like that."

"I'd be happy to teach you." That, and a whole bunch of other things.

She smiled. "Will you also teach me to ride a motorbike?"

"Did you read my mind?" I asked. Yeah, okay, it was probably obvious what I was thinking. Partly because we both knew what this time alone was for, and partly because I was a hot-blooded guy.

"I didn't need to, it's what I'm thinking too." She slipped her hand into mine and I led her away from the bike and toward the beach.

"Is that rowboat for Penn?" She smiled teasingly at me.

"Don't tell him, but yes," I joked. "We're going to use it first though."

"Are we going fishing?" she guessed.

"That depends, do you *want* to go fishing?" I asked.

She frowned slightly, like she rolled the question around in her mind before she responded. "I mean, if that's what you organised, then I'd love to." That was very diplomatic, but I couldn't tell what she was really thinking.

"And if I didn't?" I asked.

"Did you?" She was never one to hold back for long.

"No, I didn't." I grabbed the end of the boat and started to drag it towards the water. It wasn't too heavy, and slid easily over the perfect sand, leaving a gouge behind it. The tide would swallow it soon enough, making it look like we were never here.

"Thank goodness, because I hate fishing," she admitted. "I'm not very outdoorsy. I'm more of a city girl."

"Me too," I said. I paused for a moment and laughed. "Except the girl part." *Smooth, Jax*, I told myself. She probably thought I was an idiot and she hadn't known until now.

Thankfully, she laughed too, and moved to grab the end of the boat beside me.

Together, we dragged it down to the sand and into the shallows.

"Do you know how to row?" She twisted the front of her skirt in one hand and held it up out of the water.

"Would you believe I rowed competitively in high school and university?"

She regarded me for a moment. "I think I would believe that, yes. Were you any good at it?"

I took her hand and helped her to climb into the boat. "Not Olympic-level good, but not bad. Mostly it was just fun and good exercise. Then I met Levi and we started the band and I got too busy for it. Hopefully it's like riding a bike, you never forget how." I climbed in and sat facing her, my back to the front of the boat.

I gripped the oars and started to row.

She watched me for a couple of minutes then said, "It's kinda hot that you know how to do all these things. Row, ride a bike, drive a bus."

"A manager needs all sorts of different skills," I said. "Sooner or later, they come in handy. This one in particular. You never know when you might need to row a beautiful woman around on a tropical island."

I watched her when she smiled. I wasn't lying when I said she was beautiful, but when she smiled, it was like the whole universe exploded into fireworks. And the best thing? She had no idea how gorgeous she was. If she did, she'd have a bigger ego than all of Wolf Venom put together. All the bands who were here for IslandFest put together.

Instead, she was humble and sweet, but not scared of her own sexuality. Perfect.

"Just a wild guess, it doesn't come up often?" she said.

I cocked my head at her. "You know, you're right. It doesn't happen nearly as often as it should. I'll make a note and mention it to Levi the next time I talk to him."

She laughed. "So, where are we rowing to?"

"Who says we're rowing anywhere?" I asked. "We

might just be rowing for the fun of it." And it was fun, but it wasn't the point of this date.

"The lack of any food on the beach, and in this boat, suggests you're up to something," she pointed out. "And the fact we seem to be headed straight for that yacht." She nodded forward.

"Maybe it's in our way and we're about to run into it?" I suggested.

"If that's the case, then I suggest you turn *really* soon." She only looked slightly worried. She knew, after all we'd been through, that I wouldn't risk her life, not for anything.

I smiled and turned my head to gauge the distance between us and the yacht. At the last moment, I put down the oars and stood to grab a rope on the side of the bigger vessel. I pulled us in until we were hull to hull and tied the rowboat to the side of the yacht.

"Yours?" She looked impressed.

I snorted a laugh. "I wish. This is a bit above my pay packet. It belongs to the resort." It was a beautiful vessel. One day...

I checked the line was secure and gestured towards the ladder on the side of the yacht. "Ladies first."

"I don't see any ladies, but I can go first." She grinned at me and gripped the bottom rung to pull herself up. Lucky I'd told her not to wear heels, those would have gotten in the way, big time.

I watched her cute little ass and firm, inviting thighs as she climbed the ladder, then followed her.

The sun was just starting to set as we stepped onto the deck of the yacht.

"This is lovely," she said softly. Her gaze swiveled, taking everything in.

A blue tablecloth covered a table that was bolted down to the deck. The top of the table was decorated with flowers and candles. Beside the table, two boxes sat, one with food and the other with wine.

The rest of the deck was decorated with flowers and of course a wide mattress, blankets and pillows. Music played from speakers around the deck. Not hers, or Wolf Venom. The playlist was full of soft rock songs, carefully chosen to be background music, to set the scene.

Yep, classic seduction stuff. Why screw with what works?

"You thought of everything," she said.

"Probably not everything," I said. "Hopefully]enough to get us through the night." All I really needed was a little bit of food and her. Maybe not even the food.

"It's beautiful," she said.

Her tone distracted, she added, "Thank you." She

glanced around carefully, eyes narrowed in a frown. She peered below decks, into the small living area and bedroom. She might even have looked under the table.

I waited until she finished, my arms crossed over my chest. Finally, she stopped looking and nodded, satisfied.

"No sign of any evil twins?" I asked.

"Not that I can see," she said. "We might get to enjoy an uninterrupted night."

Zeke's identical twin brothers had followed us around on the entire world tour. I wouldn't be surprised if they turned up here, on the island. If they turned up on this yacht, I wouldn't hesitate to throw them back overboard. The pair did nothing but cause trouble for everyone.

We didn't call them the evil twins for nothing.

"Good, then let's have some wine and something to eat." I pulled two glasses out of the box and poured one for each of us. I handed one to her and offered her a toast.

"To not being interrupted," I said.

"I'll drink to that," she said. She raised her glass to mine and we clinked. She sipped and smiled. "Delicious."

"Not as delicious as you." I looked forward to

finding out exactly how tasty she was. Better than the wine, I'd bet.

"You're going to give me an ego the size of Penn's," she said.

I laughed. "There's no way you could have an ego that big. That's not who you are. But if you did, I'd still love you."

Her expression softened. "I love you too," she said softly. "This night is going to be perfect, I can tell."

"No pressure," I said jokingly. I slipped my arm around her.

We stood watching the sun dip toward the horizon. It glittered off the water, all pink and yellow and gold, like the world painted a special work of art just for us. The headwind that created the turbulence in the plane had dropped to just a slight breeze. The air was warm, but clear and fresh. For a little while, we could pretend we were the only two people in the entire world.

4

ABBIE

"This was incredible." I leaned back against Jackson. He wrapped his arms around me.

The yacht bobbed on water illuminated by moonlight and distant lights from a resort on the island. Every so often, the sound of distant music, and shouts of people having fun, whispered on the breeze. Aside from that, it was just us.

Being away from all the guys and the hustle and bustle of the tour was a strange but lovely change.

"I'm glad you liked it." His breath brushed the side of my neck.

I shivered deliciously.

His voice low and husky, he said, "I wasn't sure if I could compete with the other guys. You've had some memorable dates with them."

"This was memorable because it's lovely and no one has crashed it," I said.

I waited for a moment, but no evil twins appeared out of nowhere. "And because I got to spend it with you."

I turned around and wound my arms around his neck. "Also, you don't have to compete with them. I love all of you equally."

He hesitated for a moment and glanced around. "Sorry, I was waiting for Asher or Penn to say you love them the most." His teeth flashed white in the moonlight.

I laughed softly. "That is something *both* of them would say. Then they'd flip each other off."

He chuckled. "Lucky for everyone, we all get along so well. As much as I'm going to miss managing Blazing Violet, I can live without their blazing arguments. It's a miracle Violet and Blaise haven't killed each other yet."

"Or fucked each other," I said.

"Or that too. I'm sure that will happen soon enough." His grimace folded into a smile. "But let's not talk about them."

"Let's not talk at all." I pulled his mouth down to mine and kissed him lightly, barely more than a brush of my lips over his.

"I can do not talking." He kissed me more deeply,

but still soft and tasting of wine and the chocolate mousse we had for dessert.

I swept my tongue over his lips and inside his mouth to meet his.

He ran his hands up and down my back a couple of times, then slipped under the hem of my shirt. His fingers were calloused but gentle against my bare skin.

"You feel amazing." He broke off from my mouth and kissed his way down my neck, while his hands wandered up higher.

"No, you." I brought my hands down to rest lightly against his chest before I started to undo the buttons of his shirt. I hadn't seen him without one, and I was intrigued about what I would find. I expected tattoos and I wasn't disappointed. He had a dragon with outstretched wings across his chest, and several other mythological creatures on his shoulders. His chest and stomach were as firm as any of the guys', his abs clearly defined, even if he wasn't quite as ripped.

I slipped his shirt off to reveal the delicious V of his hips, and a couple more tattoos on his sides.

"What does this one mean?" I lightly touched what looked like an arrow bent into an infinity symbol, done in simple, black ink.

He glanced down. "It means sometimes you have to go through shitty times to get to good times."

I couldn't suppress a snort. "That's disturbingly accurate. Did you add, 'seeing the future,' to your list of skills?"

He smiled. "No. It's just a general rule the universe seems to have. It puts you through shit and then you come out the other side, stronger than ever." He brushed a stray bit of hair off my face. "Just like you did."

"Shame, I was going to ask if you have the numbers for next week's lottery draw," I joked. "I would have bought a ticket." Although, with seven amazing boyfriends, hadn't I already won the lottery?

He chuckled. "Sorry, I can't help you with that. I'm sure sixty-nine is one of the lucky numbers." He leaned in to kiss me again.

I laughed against his mouth. "That would be a very lucky number."

He worked his hands higher up my back and pulled my shirt up over my head. I raised my arms and broke off our kiss long enough to let him tug it off. He dropped it on the deck and unhooked my bra. After he slid that down my arms and over my hands, he stepped back to look at me.

"Holy crap, you're gorgeous," he said. "How in the

world…" He shook his head and kissed me again. His hands wandered around to my front, sliding slowly over my skin until he cupped my breasts.

"You feel even better than I imagined." He rubbed his palms up and down my nipples until they pebbled under his touch.

I hummed softly. Every touch was making me wet as hell.

"Jackson," I said just to say his name. "I want you so much."

"I want you too." He walked backward to the mattress and lay back, taking me with him. He helped me to shed the rest of my clothes and let his mouth and hands wander all over me.

He kissed his way down my body, over my stomach and down between my thighs. He slipped an arm under each one, opening me up to him.

"I've been wanting to taste you like this for so long." He lowered his mouth to my pussy and, with a feather light touch, traced circles and patterns around my clit and folds, like he was drawing musical notes with his tongue. "Just as I suspected, you're delicious."

I could only respond with a soft moan, because his delicate licks had me going crazy. I wanted more, I wanted everything, but I also wanted this to last forever.

He slowly, and as gently as he did everything, slipped a finger inside me.

"Woman, you're so wet," he said like he'd never felt anything like the inside of my body before. He added a second finger to the first, and hooked them around to massage me inside.

"Fuck, Jackson, that feels so good." I rolled my hips, bucking against his hand, wanting to feel everything, all at once, but trying not to rush.

"You really do," he agreed, his voice muffled by my pussy.

I laughed slightly, but it was cut off by a groan as pleasure built, stammering through my blood like a drum roll. "I'm going to come."

He licked and stroked me harder than ever, pushing me, driving me to the edge hard. He said something that sounded like, "Come for me, beautiful."

And I did. I came so hard my back arched and I lifted halfway off the mattress. My cry of pleasure shattered into a million different notes, which echoed across the water. They probably heard it back at the resort. Good. Let them.

I started to come down, but Jackson didn't stop. If anything, he worked me even harder than before, his determined, persistent, slow touch pushing me to another, even more explosive orgasm.

I bucked against him frantically, muscles clenching everywhere. I held my breath until I saw stars in a hundred different universes, ignited by the blood pounding through me. When I finally managed to breathe, my shout was louder than the first time. I threw back my head and screamed out his name.

I felt like I was floating down from the atmosphere, but he still didn't stop.

"One more," he said. It wasn't a suggestion. It wasn't a demand either, not exactly. It was a statement of fact. One he expected could happen, would happen.

"I don't think I can," I said. "Please—" I didn't know what I was asking for. Maybe for him to stop, and maybe begging him never to stop.

"You can," he insisted. "One more for me." His hand and mouth worked me with expert, precise touch. I was his instrument and he knew exactly how to play me. Precisely how to get my body to do what he wanted. What we both wanted.

I started to shake my head, but the pressure rose again.

It was slower this time; Adante, not allegro. A rising tide instead of a flash flood. Although I'd probably covered his hand with a flood of my juices.

When I came for a third time, his name was

ripped from my lips louder than before. So loud it left my throat almost raw. I bucked and rolled against him so hard the yacht rocked with me. Honestly, I was so lost in pleasure I didn't care. The whole world disappeared and the only thing that was left was one long, intense orgasm that swallowed me whole and slowly slithered me out the other side.

"Holy shit," I said once I finally managed to get my breath back. "That was insane."

"In a good way, I hope." He slipped his arms out from under my thighs and scooted up until he was lying beside me. He smelled of me and, when he kissed me, tasted of me.

"In a very good way." I rolled onto my side and unfastened the front of his jeans. His erection was so eager to escape, it was a miracle he hadn't broken the zipper, or split the seam of his boxers.

I blinked. My eyebrows rose.

"Okay, I wasn't expecting that."

Four bars, parallel to each other, were pierced down the length of Jackson's cock.

"Babe, you get hotter and hotter," I told him. Landon had thought about getting a Jacob's ladder, but I had no idea Jackson already had one. I lightly ran my finger across each one, and the skin in between. Both were deliciously warm to the touch.

"You know what they say, it's always the quiet ones." He grinned. He grabbed me and rolled me until I straddled his hips.

I smiled back. "They do say that, don't they? I guess when it comes to you, I need to learn to expect the unexpected." I positioned myself so my pussy was over his cock and lowered myself down slowly.

His eyes widened. "I could say the same about you." He exhaled slowly. "You feel so fucking incredible."

"So do you." His piercings massaged my insides, teasing, sliding against sensitive flesh. I definitely had at least one more orgasm in me, maybe more. He felt so ridiculously amazing, how could I not?

He gripped my hips in firm, gentle hands, but let me choose the rhythm. "I thought about this so many times, but this is at least a billion percent better than anything I imagined."

"I'm so glad I didn't disappoint you," I teased. I started slowly, rising and falling up and down his hard cock.

He laughed softly. "You could never do that. Not even if you tried." He looked up at me with a combination of bliss and love that both melted my heart and heated my core.

"I love you," I said, as the pressure slowly rose yet again.

"I love you too." He thrust up into my body, hips working. "I'm the luckiest guy in the world right now."

"I'm the luckiest girl in the world all the time." I locked my eyes on his and watched his face as I rode him, slow then fast then slow again. His piercings massaged my insides like nothing I ever felt before. As it was, his cock was big enough and thick enough to fill me to absolute ecstasy.

"Come with me," he said. "Come with me, beautiful girl."

I pressed my palms to his rock hard stomach and drove us both with deliberate rolls of my hips, in perfect rhythm with him.

My eyes not moving from his, I came harder than ever. At the same time he stilled and came inside me. In that moment, there was nothing but me and him, love and pleasure, fireworks and hot blood, release and breathless panting.

We finally slumped together on the mattress sweating and trying to catch our breath. For the longest time we just lay there tangled around each other, lost in the perfect moment.

5

ABBIE

It was still dark when I woke. Jackson and I had managed a shower before falling asleep on the mattress on deck, his arms around me.

I opened my eyes a crack. As far as I could tell, neither of us had moved. What woke me then? Specifically, what woke me that made the hairs on the back of my neck rise? Maybe it was latent paranoia after the tour, and all we dealt with.

That's in the past, I told myself. There's nothing there.

And yet, all my senses were on high alert. Something was definitely wrong.

Jackson twitched and his hand curled around my arm. He felt it too. His hand was a warning not to speak, not to move.

I squeezed his arm in return to indicate that I understood.

I trusted Jackson completely, but if anything was up, we might wish Zeke, Asher or Tully were here. They had the skills and the background to deal with all sorts of shit. Fortunately, both of us were quick learners.

I hoped.

Something bumped against the side of the yacht.

It's just the rowboat, I told myself.

Only... The rowboat was on the *other* side of the yacht. Shit.

I hardly dared to breathe.

Something moved on the side of the boat. Or some*one*. Or several someones. Whatever it was, it probably wasn't a friendly dolphin come to hang out with us. It could be the other guys, fed up of waiting for us to come back. It would be like them to crash this party. If they did, I would...

"He's up there," a male voice said. Not one I knew. On the upside, it wasn't the evil twins. On the downside, it wasn't any of the guys either.

Wait, did he say 'he'? Were they after one of us, or was it a case of mistaken identity?

I twisted around enough to whisper in Jackson's ear. "We need to get out of here."

I barely finished speaking when the night was lit

up by a burst of light. I threw my hand up in front of my eyes and blinked like crazy.

"What the fuck—"

"It's him all right," a voice growled.

Jackson sat up, also shielding his eyes from the light. "Who are you and what the hell do you want?" He pulled me behind him, placing himself between me and whoever the fuck it was.

Another voice said. "We'll take her too. You have thirty seconds to get dressed or you're going like that."

"She looks fine just how she is," the first voice said. "Easier to have some fun with her before—"

"She's not going to live long enough for any fun," the second voice snapped.

I looked over Jackson, my eyes wild. Rule number one of any kidnapping or potential kidnapping: don't let them take you to another location.

On the other hand, the sound of a cocking gun was loud so close to my ear. Holy fucking shit.

I grabbed my clothes, which were still scattered around the deck, and dressed with about five seconds to spare. Go me.

Jackson did the same, but still managed to keep himself between me and...whoever they were. That was a very Jackson thing to do, protecting someone he cared about. He did the same with the guys in the past. He always joked he was just being a good manager, but he was more than that. He was a good guy. One of the best.

"Get in the boat," the first man ordered. He waved us over to the side of the yacht, a gun in his hand.

"I feel like if you're going to kidnap us, you should at least tell us who you are," I said. That seemed only fair to me, although I doubted they were going to be that forthcoming. People didn't sneak up on you in the night and then tell you all about themselves. Right?

"You'll find out soon enough," he said.

"Okay, well... For the record, I hate being kidnapped. It's getting to be really annoying." I swung a leg over the side of the yacht and started down the ladder on the opposite side to the rowboat.

"I agree," Jackson said. "Being kidnapped sucks. You could just tell us what you want. Maybe we can work something out. It sounds like it's me you want anyway. Leave her here. She—"

"We want you to shut up," the second voice snapped predictably. Whoever they were, they weren't chatty. Honestly, I didn't want their life story anyway, just the reason they were doing this and what they wanted from us. It might be something we could resolve over leftover lobster. Oh, right, we ate it all. There might be some bread left.

"We don't need you with all your body parts intact," the first man said.

Since I preferred to have my body parts intact, I pressed my lips together and fell silent.

I stepped down to a boat bigger than the rowboat but smaller than the yacht. Another man grabbed me around the waist and pushed me onto a seat. Jackson was plopped down beside me a moment later.

"Please tell me this was part of the date," I whispered. "Just to spice things up a bit." I wasn't sure if I'd be relieved or pissed off if that was the case. He might earn himself a one way trip overboard.

"No," he whispered back. "Should it be? I could have—"

"Fuck no," I said quickly. "Everything was perfect up until now. Any idea who they are?"

He looked thoughtful. "I'm hoping there's a competing festival who really, really wanted you to sing there."

"The chance of that seems kinda slim," I pointed out.

He sighed. "Really slim. My other guess is much worse. "

"Please tell me your other guess is a rival *label*," I joked weakly. "I'll also accept a practical joke." Since they seemed to know who he was, mistaken identity was probably off the table.

"It's more likely they have to do with one of our families," Jackson admitted. "Unless you accidentally pissed someone off recently?"

"If I did, you'd know," I said.

"That's true." Nothing happened that he and Levi Jones didn't know about, or find out about pretty quickly. Or know before the rest of us knew. Or— Yeah, they were well informed.

The first two kidnappers jumped into the boat and a man moved to start the engine and peel us away from the yacht.

We sat in silence for a few minutes, until I said, "As soon as the guys notice we're missing, they'll come after us."

"Yeah," Jackson said. "They—"

The kidnapper piloting the boat picked up something from beside the steering controls and pointed it over his shoulder towards the yacht.

A couple of seconds passed and nothing happened.

Then the yacht exploded into a huge fireball that lit up the night and all the water around it. Flames and debris flew into the sky. The blast sent huge waves that threatened to swamp the boat we were on. We crested one and slid down the other side. My stomach made approximately the same motion and I groaned.

Jackson gripped the seat in front of him with one hand and me with the other, while I held onto the seat with both hands, knuckles white.

"Worst carnival ride ever," I growled. Thank fuck Penn wasn't here, he'd probably be throwing up already. I was close to doing it myself.

"This is bullshit," I said once the ocean settled again. Tears ran down my cheeks at the sight of the yacht. It quickly burnt down to the waterline. "What if they think we died on there?" The yacht was going to be on the bottom of the ocean within an hour or two. By the time they brought it back up to the surface, if they did, and realised we weren't there, days could have gone by. Or longer.

"Hey." Jackson put an arm around my shoulders and pulled me to him. "You have met them, right? They'll figure it out. And you know us, we're resourceful. We're badasses. We've gotten ourselves out of worse situations than this, and we've done it in style. Well, you've done it in style, I'm just the manager."

"You're very stylish," I said firmly. "And you're not just the manager. You're one of my boyfriends and a guy I love." He was right though, we had gotten ourselves out of some terrible situations, but we'd had all the other guys with us, and all their skills. This time, it was just the two of us and I didn't even have a pair of heels to stab someone in the eyeball with. If it came to it, that was. It seemed kindly likely that it might. This was so fucked up.

"I love you too." He pressed his nose to mine.

"We told you to shut up," one of the kidnappers growled. "Maybe we should separate them."

"Just keep an eye on them, Leopold," the man piloting the boat said. "As long as they cooperate, we have no need to make this unpleasant."

"Yes, Nikolai," Leopold grunted. He didn't look happy at being told not to throw his weight around.

Me, on the other hand... I nodded towards Nikolai. "I like this guy. I mean, for a kidnapper, he seems kinda reasonable. Don't you think?"

Jackson shrugged one shoulder. "I've been kidnapped by worse."

"Actually, so have I," I said. "How about that?"

Nikolai turned and gave us a funny look. He probably thought we were completely insane.

Maybe we were, but this was how we dealt with stress around here. We made silly jokes and kept things as light as we could.

"Any idea where they're taking us?" I whispered.

Jackson shook his head lightly. "Another yacht or another island would be my guess, but I could be wrong. For all I know, they might have a submarine around here somewhere."

"I've always wanted to go in a submarine, but not against my will," I remarked.

"Really?" Jackson asked. "I can't say it's on my bucket list." He scratched the back of his head. "They seem like they're all about really enclosed spaces and underwater and all that shit. But if you want to do that someday, I'll see if I can organise something. The other guys might want to go too."

"I bet they would," I agreed. "We could have a band outing on a submarine." Of course, we had to live long enough to do it.

"Is there anything else you want me to organise?" he asked. "Just, you know, while we're on the subject."

I thought about that for a moment. "I've always wanted to go in a hot air balloon. I hear they have really nice ones over Canberra." If I remembered right, they flew at sunrise over the small Australian capital. It sounded beautiful and serene. I could use a bit of serenity right now.

"That should be easy to arrange. I'll pencil that in. When I get a pencil." He looked like there were other things he wanted to do with that pencil, namely shoving it into the eyeball of Leopold or one of the others.

"You're the best," I said. "I bet Asher would be ecstatic if you organise a skydive too."

"I wonder if Penn would jump," Jackson mused.

"If the others do, then he definitely will," I said. Penn wouldn't let his fear get in the way of his ego, even if he was shit scared.

"That's true," Jackson said. He squinted up ahead at the rising sun.

I looked in the same direction but didn't see anything but open waters. Wherever we were going, this could be a long boat ride. At least they didn't make us row. Yeah, that's me, thinking about all the important things. Whatever got us through the next couple of days. And kept me from freaking the fuck out.

6

ZEKE

"Can't sleep?" Asher flopped down on the sand beside me and sat with his arms around his bent knees.

I glanced over at him. My oldest friend, and now boyfriend, I couldn't remember a time when he wasn't a big part of my life. Once in a while, we talked about what we would have done if we hadn't formed a band. Whatever it was, we would have done it together.

"Neither can you, by the look of it, babe." I looked back towards the dark waves. The sun would be up soon, but for now there was only moonlight and pathway lights to illuminate the resort. It was beautiful, but I was too on edge to appreciate it right now.

"Looking over our shoulders is an ingrained

habit," he said. "I'm not sure I can outgrow it, as much as I want to."

Those were my thoughts as well, but there was something else. Call it a sixth sense, instinct, whatever. Something was wrong. Or I was being paranoid.

"I shouldn't have let them go out there by themselves," I said.

"Firstly, I don't think you could have stopped them," he said. "Secondly, you know where they are?"

"I made Jackson tell me before they left, in case something happened." He wasn't happy about it, but he understood. I planned to be too careful for a long time. Possibly forever. Whatever it took to keep us all safe, even if it meant overstepping a whole lot.

"They're on a yacht out there." I waved in a vague direction.

"And now you think something's happened?" Asher asked. "What is it?" He didn't question my instincts, or tell me I was crazy. He got me. He'd also grown up in a mobster family. And he knew when I thought something was up, it was. I'd never been wrong yet. I hoped like hell I was wrong this time.

I shook my head. "I don't know. It might be nothing more than Abbie breaking a nail."

"But it might also be that Jackson fell overboard and got eaten by a shark," Asher said lightly.

"That would be bad," I said. "But we would have heard Abbie screaming from here if that happened. Unless it ate her too."

"Talking about eating her makes my cock hard," Asher commented.

"What doesn't make your cock hard?" I teased.

"Thinking about pineapple." He dug his toes into the sand. "I don't know how people can eat that stuff."

"Because it's delicious?" I suggested.

"You're delicious." He leaned his shoulder against me and rested his head against mine.

"That's funny, I was going to say the same about you." I sighed softly and took a moment to enjoy the way it felt to sit here like this with him. It was almost enough to put my nerves to rest. With a hint of breeze and the sound of the waves lapping on the beach, it was peaceful here.

"You're right about that, I am," he said jokingly. "We should go to resorts like this more often. It's nice to sit here doing nothing and not think about too much. Live in the moment and all that stuff."

"It is nice," I agreed. "I love you, babe."

"I love you too." He nestled in a little closer. "You know what would make this perfect?"

"What's that?" I asked.

"If—"

The night exploded.

A bang echoed across the waves. A fireball flew into the sky. The yacht, previously invisible in the dark, was now lit up like a bonfire.

I shot to my feet, almost knocking Asher aside.

"Fuck!"

He got to his feet. "Please don't tell me that's where…"

"Of course it fucking is," I said. "We need to get out there." A hand on the back of my head, I looked around frantically. Between the burning yacht and the rising sun, there was enough light to see a lot of sand and no boats. No jet skis. Not even an inflatable hippo.

"The surfboard shed is—" Asher raised his hand to point.

"It will have to do." I headed off at a run, him on my heels.

We passed the villa door just as it opened and a sleepy Penn stuck his head out, Tully right behind him.

"What the hell, dude?" Penn asked.

"Get the others and come with us," I shouted as I bolted past. I didn't need to look back to see if they did what I told them to. I knew they would. This wasn't our first rodeo, as they say.

I sprinted to the surfboard storage shed and

grabbed hold of the handle. I tugged, but it was locked.

I swore under my breath. Of course it was locked, but the door didn't look very sturdy. I took a step back and kicked the door in. The door frame splintered, parting it from the lock easily. It was the kind of security only designed to keep out honest people, not to keep desperate people from breaking in. They could send me the bill for the repairs later. I might recommend an upgrade, if they didn't want people helping themselves to surfboards.

I grabbed the closest board and swung it around, almost throwing it at Asher. I didn't stop to see if he caught it before I grabbed another and tucked it under my arm.

We stepped out of the shed when the other four guys arrived. Without more than a quick, questioning glance, they stepped past and grabbed their own boards. I made a mental note to thank them all later for not wasting time asking what the fuck was going on.

Asher was right beside me as I hit the water, board out in front of me, and started to paddle. It was a long time since I'd been surfing, but I'd done enough of it to move quickly through the water. I kept my eyes open, looking for any sign of Abbie and

Jackson in the water, or the sharks we'd joked about minutes earlier.

None of that seemed funny anymore.

I cursed myself for not going out to the yacht sooner. I fucking knew something was up. If I acted when my instincts first twitched, I might have prevented this. Whatever *this* was. Yeah, okay, I might also have gotten caught up in it. The speculation was pointless, so I pushed it aside.

The yacht still burned ferociously. It sat heavier now, sinking towards the water line as it got more and more swamped. There was no sign of Jackson or Abbie treading water. No floating bodies. If they were on that yacht when it exploded…

No, I couldn't think like that. They were fine. They had to be. If they weren't, I was not going to be okay. And if someone did this to them, I was going to rip their heads off and shove it up their asses.

"There's a rowboat." Asher pointed.

I followed the line of his gesture and nodded. He was right. The small craft floated maybe twenty metres from the burning yacht, bobbing on the swell.

I turned my board and started to paddle toward it

"Abbie?" I called out. "Jackson?" I couldn't see anyone in the rowboat, no movement or sound. It wasn't until I reached the side and peered in, that I saw it was empty. A length of rope trailed in the water. I grabbed it and hauled it up. The end was singed. It must have burned through letting the boat drift away.

"Fuck." I flung the rope away and turned back towards the yacht.

The sun was a finger above the horizon by now. If Jackson or Abbie were anywhere nearby, we'd be able to see them.

Unless...

I paddled faster towards the yacht. A glance back over my shoulder showed the other guys right behind me. They all looked as worried and scared as I felt. Landon, in particular, looked like he was ready to pee his pants. Like always, he stayed close to Channing.

"We'll find them," Asher said.

I looked over at him and nodded. "Hell yeah, we will."

Closer to the yacht, the heat was more intense. I ignored it and kept paddling until I reached the side. I grabbed hold of an un-burnt section and pulled myself over and onto the deck.

"Zeke? Is that a good idea?" Asher asked.

I glanced back. "Probably not, but someone has to do it. Stay there and keep an eye out for them." I looked away before I could see whether he nodded or not.

A hand in front of my face to shield my eyes from the heat, I stepped carefully. The yacht wobbled dangerously underneath me. If I wasn't careful, someone would die on board. Me. Hard pass.

I saw what looked like the edge of a blanket and the remains of a mattress to the side of the deck. Near that was what might have been a phone an hour or so ago. Now, it was a twisted piece of metal and plastic.

There was absolutely no sign of Abbie or Jackson. No remains, no stink of burning meat. Nothing.

I turned around slowly, taking in everything, before I stepped back to the twisted railing. Wincing from walking on the hot deck, I slipped into the water. In a few strokes I reached my board and reclaimed it from Asher, who had hung on to it with one hand.

"They're not there," I said. "If I had to guess, I would say they were gone before that exploded."

"Not a coincidence then," Tully remarked. He looked the yacht over with all the attention I'd given it. If I missed anything, he'd pick it up.

Asher too. He seemed as though he was nothing more than a jokester, but he was as meticulous and observant as me. He likes to say that no one suspects a drummer who's always laughing and messing around, and he wasn't wrong. It got him places the rest of us couldn't go. Trust that wouldn't be bestowed on me. People liked to confide in him. Some regretted it later.

"Empty yachts don't usually explode by themselves," I said. "Someone did this. Whoever it was, they probably thought we'd assume Abbie and Jackson are dead and not go after them."

"Or this is a distraction," Tully said. "They wanted us out here."

"What the fuck for?" Penn snarled. "Some up and coming band wants our spot in IslandFest?"

"Fuck that," Channing said.

"What he said," Landon agreed.

"I know some people get desperate to be famous, but this is going too far," I said.

"You don't think that's what this is though, do you?" Asher asked.

"Not for a moment," I said. "I think someone took them, and we're going to get them back."

"Of course we are," Asher agreed.

"Definitely." Landon nodded. "Where do we start?" He looked at me with absolute trust that I had all the answers.

That would be great if I had any. Right then, I was drawing a blank.

"We need to get back to the resort and let the authorities deal with the yacht," I said. "Then we'll figure things out." I hoped, because I didn't know who would have done this.

Rattling around in my brain was a few possibilities, but I ruled most of them out one by one. That left a very small list. Even a small list was better than nothing.

"Can't the universe give us a mother fucking break?" Penn snarled.

"At least life is never boring," Tully said with a sigh. If he was trying to pretend he wasn't as worried as the rest of us, he failed. I knew him too well for that. As well as he knew me, so when he looked at me and gave a slight nod, I knew he wasn't fooled by my calm façade either.

"I'd like some fucking boring." Penn kicked to turn his board around and started back to shore.

"Me too," I said to his back. "Me too."

7

ABBIE

"Nice place for a resort." If I had to guess, I'd say we were on the boat for at least two hours. We passed a few other watercraft, but never got too close.

Each time, Leopold or one of the other kidnappers—George or Nikolai—would point a gun at us, and remind us that calling out for help was a bad idea.

Personally, I thought it was a great idea, unless it got us, or any potential rescuers, killed. Then it was a really crappy idea. If only to keep anyone innocent from being dragged into this insanity, I said nothing, but it chafed.

Eventually, a purple bruise appeared on the horizon. It soon became a small landmass, then an island. One which looked unoccupied until we followed the shoreline around to a bay, which held a small building and a dock. Both of them looked relatively new.

"Or a private tropical home," Jackson said. "We should bring the guys here and see if they want to buy it. It would be a nice place to drop out of civilisation."

"It really would," I agreed. Since Nikolai was the most reasonable kidnapper up until this point, I said to him, "Did you bring us all the way here just to show us a nice island we can buy? Because you could have just asked."

"Can we kill them now?" Leopold asked. "She's a mouthy bitch."

I had a few words which would describe him perfectly, but I decided not to share them, on the grounds they might get me killed. I'd save them so I could insult Penn with them later. He'd get a chuckle out of them. Or he'd tell me to fuck off, and to get on my knees and suck his cock. Which I would happily do. Our relationship was complicated.

"Not yet," Nikolai said.

George hopped out of the boat onto the dock and tied up the vessel before the rest of us got off. Nikolai led the way off the dock and up a path that led through some trees. The rest of the kidnappers walked behind us, Leopold with a grumpy scowl on his face. He seemed like the kind of man who needed to kill someone before breakfast, or he couldn't start his day.

I preferred coffee.

The trees opened to a section of lawn which led to a long, low house overlooking the ocean.

"I've seen enough movies to think this looks like the lair of a supervillain," I said. I glanced over at Jackson when he didn't laugh or agree. For the first time since we met, he looked tense. And I'd seen him when someone was holding a gun to his head. This was more than fear. He looked as though he knew exactly what was going on. And he didn't like it.

"Is this where you tell me exactly what's going on?" I whispered.

"I don't know exactly what's going on," he said slowly.

"But you have a reasonable idea, right?" I cocked my head at him and silently begged him to give me some answers.

"Yeah," he agreed reluctantly.

"And it's not good, is it?" Okay, I knew that already. Nice people didn't kidnap others at gunpoint. Not without their consent anyway.

"No. I apologise in advance for getting you dragged into this." He shot me a look of regret.

"What is *this?*"

"You'll find out soon enough," Nikolai said over his shoulder.

"I've always hated cryptic crosswords," I said. "Because I hate cryptic *anything*. If you're going to kill me, the least you can do is tell me why." Okay, the least they could do was tell me nothing and just kill me, but if I didn't get any answers I would find a way to haunt all of them, including Jackson.

None of them said a word.

They marched us up to the front of the house and in through a side door.

I was expecting a compound inside. Maybe some torture devices, or a man sitting in a chair stroking a fluffy white cat.

Instead, it was an ordinary, if tastefully decorated, island home. Hardwood floors, wicker furniture, lots of shiplap on the walls. Everything was white, blue or oatmeal coloured. There wasn't even a single person chained to the wall, or a table covered with a map and plans for world domination.

Okay, I admit it, I was slightly disappointed.

In spite of that I said, "I like what they've done with the place. It just screams Caribbean relaxation. Doesn't it?" I watched Jackson carefully. His eyes were on the door down the end of the house.

"You've been here before?" I asked him.

His tongue slid over his lips, a sure sign of nerves.

"Not for a long time, but yes."

"Sit down." Nikolai waved to a couch which faced a window.

The view was incredible, but I was in no mood to appreciate it. Right now, I was too scared, and getting more so by the minute.

I sat, but didn't take my eyes off Jackson. It occurred to me how little I really knew about him. I knew he was my manager and Wolf Venom's manager. I knew he was a longtime friend of Levi Jones. I knew he was the bass player for Levi and the Rips—which as band names went, was pretty epic. I knew he knew about the guys' gangster families and didn't bat an eye at any of it. I knew the sight of disembodied heads made him vomit.

He wasn't alone in the last one.

Apart from those things, and the fact he could row and drive a bus, what else did I know? It never occurred to me for a moment that he might come from the same background as most of the guys. Or worse.

I loved him, but I felt like I was looking at a stranger. One who seemed to be trying to keep himself from unravelling around the edges.

"It's me you want," Jackson said softly. "Take

Abbie back to the island. She has to be there for IslandFest. They're going to notice her absence."

"I'm not going without you," I said firmly. In spite of everything, he was still one of my guys and I wasn't walking away and leaving him here.

"If we don't need her, then we can kill her," Leopold growled.

"I'd like you a lot more if you stopped talking about killing me," I told him. I already knew they weren't going to take me back, not after all their effort to bring me here in the first place.

"Also, I think you do need me. If you didn't, I'd be dead right now." That begged the question, what did they need me for?

Yeah, okay, I could figure that one out. If this was about Jackson, then I was here for leverage. Oh goody. Although, that meant we weren't completely powerless. Right?

Jackson rubbed his forehead with his fingertips. "It's probably best you don't antagonise them any further. Let me do the talking. I'll do the best I can to get you out of here safely."

"Not without you," I said again.

He turned his face to look at me past his fingers. "You might not have a choice. If you get the chance to get out of here, you need to take it. No matter what happens to me. Promise me."

"Jackson—"

His denim blue eyes looked right at me, like he was trying to see into my soul. "Promise me," he insisted. "We don't both need to die."

"You're not—" I started. I sighed in frustration. "Okay, I promise. If I can get out of here I can, but if we can both get out of here, then that's what we'll do."

He nodded, but he didn't look convinced that would happen. Honestly, I wasn't too convinced either.

"Who owns this place?" I asked. "If there's any chance of us buying it, we should at least have some idea of its history." Okay, it might give me a clue as to what the fuck was going on too.

As expected, no one answered me. I decided to take Jackson's advice and be quiet for a while. I'd spent enough time with the other guys to know that sometimes you need to listen and watch in order to figure out what's going on and what to do.

I made a note of all the entrances and exits, the windows and the furnishings, and the way our kidnappers stood around us. Even if they weren't armed, we were outnumbered. I knew how to use a gun if I could get my hands on one, but I had nothing in the way of hand to hand combat skills and nothing more than basic self-defence. The guys promised to teach me more when we got back to Sydney, but that wasn't for another week.

The kitchen probably held knives, but those were no good against guns.

I sighed out my nose in frustration and sat against the back of the couch, my legs crossed at my knees.

What were the rest of the guys doing right now? They wouldn't have missed the yacht exploding. Zeke should know we're not that easy to kill, but then what? How would he and the other guys know where to find us or even where to start looking?

They wouldn't, I admitted to myself. They saved me from a few things early in the tour, but as it went along, I got the confidence to save myself. I was going to have to do that now. Jackson and I, we'd have to find a way out of here and back to the guys.

If there was anything I learnt in life it was that sooner or later an opportunity would arise. I'd have to be ready to take it. Of course, it would be a lot easier if I had a fucking clue what we were up against. The odds this was a practical joke was getting slimmer by the hour.

Just in case, I glanced around for hidden cameras. Or obvious ones. I saw no sign of either. Shame, I would have enjoyed flipping them off and telling whoever was behind them to fuck the fucking fuck off. If there was anything I hated more than cryptic crosswords, it was practical jokes. Especially ones that involved guns and kidnapping. This would make a great adventure holiday experience, but in reality it sucked all kinds of hard.

The door at the end of the house, finally, opened.

Beside me, Jackson's whole body tensed even more. That was saying something, because he was pretty damn tense to start with. At least he wasn't shouting or trading insults with the kidnappers like Penn would have been.

Tully probably would have killed them all by now and they wouldn't have seen him coming. Asher would have tried to make them laugh and probably got himself killed with too many silly jokes.

I could only guess what Landon and Channing would have done, except that Channing would do anything to protect Landon, even if it meant spreading kidnapper blood all over the house. People had different ways of expressing their love for other people.

As for Zeke, he wouldn't have let them take us to begin with. He probably would have pulled a couple of guns up from under the mattress and shot them before they stepped on deck of the yacht. Yeah, that was a hot mental image. I might cling to that for a while to keep myself sane.

Jackson rose when a heavyset man stepped out of the doorway. He held out a hand to indicate that I should stay sitting.

"Jasha," the man greeted, rubbing his hands together. He started speaking rapidly in what sounded like Russian. Jackson seemed to understand every word.

I stared at him. Who the hell was he?

8

ABBIE

Jackson ran a hand over his face and shook his head. "Not a chance, Yuri. And it's Jackson. I left the other life behind a long time ago."

I was done sitting down and shutting up. I rose to my feet and looked from one guy to the other. "What's going on? I didn't know you could speak Russian."

Yuri looked at me, his eyelids heavy under bushy brows. To Jackson he said, "You should explain. A woman like her isn't the kind to back down."

"You're right, I don't." I also didn't like the suggestion he had a clue about me after sixty seconds, but whatever. "Someone should explain to me why we got kidnapped at gunpoint by someone who seems to know you." Was this the fourth time now, or the fifth? The fact I was starting to lose count was not okay.

The part where Jackson could speak Russian was kinda hot, but the rest sucked.

"It's a long story," Jackson said wearily.

"Let me guess. Bratva? KGB? Russian royalty?" I knew they didn't have one anymore, but if Jackson was a motherfucking prince, I was going to lose my mind.

Yuri chuckled. "She is something else."

"I am, aren't I? Maybe you shouldn't kill me then." That seemed reasonable to me.

"That depends on Jackson," Yuri said unhelpfully.

"Jackson doesn't want me dead."

"No, I don't," he agreed.

"Then we have a deal," Yuri stated.

"We definitely do not," Jackson said.

"If you start at the beginning of the long story, you might get to the end sooner or later," I said. Otherwise, I might skip over to the kitchen and look for a knife. At this point, I wasn't sure who I would use it on.

"Would you like some coffee?" Yuri offered.

"I'd love some." That was the most civilised thing anyone said all day. "As long as it's not poisoned."

Yuri waved at the couch. "Sit. Make yourselves comfortable. Jackson can tell you everything."

"Yeah, someone needs to." And let's face it, he was the only one here I trusted to tell me the truth.

I perched on the edge of the couch and crossed my arms.

He sat down heavily beside me. "You probably guessed by now my family is Russian. They moved to Australia when I was five and changed our name to Beckett. They wanted to put the past behind them. My mother worked in a bakery but my father worked for the government. Specifically, getting intelligence on other world governments."

I blinked. "Your father was a spy? That's kinda cool."

He snorted softly. "Yeah, kinda. One of those other governments didn't think it was very cool though. They put a price on his head, so we had to run. My father's former employers kept track of us. He was one of the best they had and they wanted him to go back eventually. He refused. Australia was a lot safer. He got a job driving a bus. He was happy."

"Was?" I echoed.

"Somehow, someone from Bratva found out who he was and where he was, so my parents went into hiding. Yuri wants to know where they are."

"Why?" I looked over to Yuri, who was leaning against the kitchen bench, waiting for the coffee machine to heat up.

"Because his whereabouts are worth a lot of money," Yuri said. "What Jackson didn't tell you is that his father was a double agent and an enforcer. His loyalty was not to Russia either. He tortured a lot of innocent people for enjoyment."

"So he pissed off a lot of people?" I guessed. "And a lot of people want him dead."

"I don't want him dead," Yuri said. "I want to collect the bounty on his whereabouts. What happens to him after that..." He shrugged his broad shoulders.

"I'm guessing that's a lot since you've gone to all this trouble," I said.

"Several million dollars," Yuri said. "I even offered to share some of it with Jackson."

"Just a wild guess here, but he told you to fuck off?" I looked back at Jackson as he nodded.

"He did some shitty things, but he's still my father."

"Of course he is." We'd covered up plenty of dubious things over the last couple of months, what was one more?

"Let me get this straight," I said slowly. "If you tell this asshole where your father is, your father ends up dead. But if you don't, then he's going to kill me? That's why I'm here, isn't it? They need you alive, or they won't find out where he is." That was awesome, wasn't it now?

Fuck.

"If they kill you, I'm definitely not going to cooperate," Jackson said firmly.

"We don't need to kill her to get you to cooperate." Yuri poured a coffee and took a sip. "Mmmm, this is good."

"You're going to torture us by withholding coffee?" I asked. "You're more evil than you look." What kind of asshole does that?

"I'll start by withholding coffee. Where it finishes is up to you. But don't think you have to decide now. I'll give you a couple of hours to talk about it. I'm sure your woman is very persuasive."

Talk about putting me in an impossible situation. I didn't want to die or be tortured, but asking Jackson to give up his father's whereabouts was a whole other story.

"Leopold, Nikolai, take our guests to the guest suite," Yuri said. "Leopold, don't kill anyone until I tell you to. And don't hurt them either. You'll get your chance soon enough if they decide not to cooperate."

Leopold didn't look happy at that, but he nodded and waved his gun at us. He really did seem to enjoy that part of his job. I wondered if he was a bully at school too.

Nikolai, being slightly less of an asshole, gestured with his hand. "This way."

They led us through the door Yuri had come through, and into a corridor at the back of the house.

Nikolai opened a door and nodded for us to step inside.

I glanced at Jackson, who also nodded. He looked at least as troubled as I felt, but seemed inclined to cooperate with them for now.

I shrugged and stepped into the room, Jackson right behind me.

Nikolai pulled the door shut and I heard the lock click into place.

"Well this is great," I said with a deep sigh. My brain was twisting and turning in a million different directions and none of them were good.

The room was as tastefully decorated as the rest of the house, with a wide bed and windows overlooking the ocean, but it was still a cell.

I stepped over to a window and looked out. "I was hoping to see a fleet of ships, with Zeke standing at the front like that scene in *Titanic*. But maybe armed. To the teeth. With rocket launchers." Instead, all I saw was empty sea.

Bummer.

Jackson walked up behind me and wound his arms around me. "I'm sorry you got caught up in this. I haven't heard from them for months. I thought they'd given up. I should have known they wouldn't."

I leaned my head back against his chest.

"When it comes to money, people tend to be persistent. Why does he need it if he owns this place?" The island alone would be worth more than five million dollars.

"He probably doesn't," Jackson said. "It's borrowed, or maybe the owner doesn't know he's here."

"We can add breaking and entering to his list of crimes." It was a minor felony compared to kidnapping and threats of torture and murder.

"And withholding coffee," he said.

"That might be the worst thing of all," I joked weakly. Honestly, I could give up coffee for the rest of my life if it meant I didn't get tortured or killed. It was a small thing in the scheme of things.

"At least we have a view," he remarked. "He could have locked us away in a room without one."

"He's completely redeemed then," I said sarcastically. "This would have been a lot easier if you were a prince."

"This would be a lot easier if my father wasn't who he was," Jackson said. "That includes being a king. Although, I think I'd make a pretty crappy prince. I'm not a big fan of publicity or cutting ribbons."

"Yeah, that doesn't sound like you at all," I said. "Plus they would have wanted you to marry a princess. One who doesn't have six other boyfriends."

"In some cultures, that would be exactly who they'd want me to marry," he said. "A warrior princess with six warrior boyfriends to protect me. That sounds pretty perfect to me."

"Princess Abigail," I said. "That does have a ring to it. Are you sure you're not secretly royalty?"

He chuckled. "I'm pretty sure I'm not. Does it matter?"

I pretended to think about that for a moment. "I suppose it doesn't. Unless it would mean an army is coming to rescue us. Otherwise, I'm okay with being ordinary, and being with you, manager, bass player Jackson." I looked over my shoulder at him and smiled. "I love you."

"I love you too." He kissed my cheek. "But there's nothing ordinary about you. You're my smart, gorgeous, amazing, talented girlfriend. I'm beyond lucky to know you."

I turned back to the window and sighed. "So if there isn't an army of your loyal subjects, or a fleet captained by Zeke, then what are we going to do? Do you really know where your father is?"

"Sort of," he said. "Not his exact location, but I could find him if I had to."

I realised by his cagey response that he assumed someone was listening in. That made sense. They might have hoped we were dumb enough to give them answers by accident.

Nice try, assholes, I thought. They were going to have to try harder than that. Or better yet, let us go and forget about it all. That sounded like a good idea to me.

"Am I really supposed to ask you to tell them where he is, just to save my own ass?" How could I possibly ask Jackson to choose between me and his father? That was an impossible choice, even if he did horrible things in the past. It wasn't as though I was perfect either.

"That's exactly what most people would do," he said. "I wouldn't blame you if you did. Why should you go through all of this for someone you don't know?"

"Why should you go through this for someone you *do* know?" I asked. "This won't come as a surprise to you, but some people suck."

He laughed bitterly. "Yeah, they do. But people like you and me, we're tough. We'll get through this."

"I hope so, because I don't want to die on a tropical island, kilometres from anywhere, and have my remains thrown to the sharks to cover up my death." That would be absolute bullshit if it happened. I would definitely haunt them if they did that to me.

"That's why we're going to get out of here," Jackson whispered. "If you're ready to leave, that is?"

"I'm very ready to get the hell out of here," I whispered back. "But how?"

"Do you trust me?"

9

ABBIE

"I've decided to talk," Jackson stated.

He'd knocked on the door until Nikolai unlocked it and opened it. Both he and Leopold looked at him doubtfully. Leopold, in particular, looked pissed off. Presumably he'd miss out on his fun if Jackson cooperated and gave up his father.

If he felt that strongly about hurting people, there were three other kidnappers and Yuri on this island. He had my blessing to kill any of them. In fact, he'd be doing us a favour.

I considered suggesting it but figured he'd probably decline my kind offer. His loss.

"Come this way then," Nikolai said. He stepped back from the door and kept his gun on us while we walked out of the room. "I suggest you don't waste Yuri's time. He's a very busy man."

He couldn't be that busy if he had time for kidnapping and threatening innocent people. I kept that thought to myself. Jackson suggested I not speak, but keep my eyes and ears open and let him do the talking. Whatever it took to get us out of here alive, I'd happily do it.

We walked back out to the kitchen and living area. Yuri was sitting on a couch reading a book. I liked to think people who read weren't too evil, but I'd more or less been proven wrong about that in the past. Besides, I knew that book. I read it a year or two ago. One of the guys likes to torture people for fun. He could have been looking for inspiration in the pages.

"I hear you're ready to speak," Yuri said without looking up. "I should tell you, even if you do divulge your father's location, I intend to keep you here until the information is confirmed as correct."

"That doesn't work for me," Jackson said. "I'll give you the information you want and then you let us go."

Now Yuri looked up. "It's adorable that you think this is a negotiation. It's not. In case you hadn't noticed, I hold all the cards."

"Except the one with my father's location written on it," Jackson said. "I think they call that the ace card or something." He glanced over at me but I shrugged.

I had no idea about cards. It sounded about right though.

"If I kill her, he might realise we're not playing games," Leopold said. He sounded way too excited at the idea.

I forced my gaze over to the setting sun, visible through the window. It was beautiful, and helped me to remember to keep my mouth shut when I wanted to tell Leopold to fuck off.

Yuri clicked his tongue. "Leopold has some anger issues, but he's loyal."

I swung my eyes back to see Leopold give Yuri a glare that didn't look particularly loyal to me. I had a sneaking suspicion he'd happily put a bullet in his boss's brain just to satisfy the urge.

Do it. Do it.

Unfortunately, he didn't.

"It shouldn't take more than a day or two to confirm your information," Yuri said. "If you're being honest, you might get back in time for your little festival."

Little festival? I choked back a response. He might be a reader, but he clearly had no idea about musical events. That moved him up a notch on my scale of evil. On the other hand, I suspected he knew exactly what IslandFest was, and he was trying to get a rise from me.

"Your girlfriend is quiet all of a sudden." Yuri cocked his head at me. "Nothing to say, little wildcat? I bet you love leaving scratch marks all over dear Jackson here."

I couldn't stop myself. I said, "Him and my other six boyfriends."

His eyebrows shot up. Then he laughed. "You really are quite the woman. Maybe I should keep you here when Jackson leaves."

Jackson bristled visibly. "Not a chance. You couldn't handle her anyway."

"That sounds like a challenge to me," Yuri said. "Unfortunately, my wife would not approve. I'm so sorry to disappoint you, dear."

"I'll try to contain my heartbreak," I said sarcastically.

"So, do you want to know where my father is or don't you?" Jackson asked. "Because if you don't, we'll be on our way." He made to step toward the door we'd come in through.

"Nikolai, take down the details," Yuri said. To Jackson he said, "Know this. If the information is wrong, I'll start by having Leopold remove your girlfriend's tongue. Then one breast, and then the other.

Then he can decide if he wants to remove her fingers or her toes one by one."

"Fingers are more fun," Leopold said.

"You're a sick fuck," I told him.

He actually grinned at me. Apparently the idea of cutting me up into little pieces appealed to him.

Honestly, the idea of cutting him up into little pieces was sounding more and more enticing. Just the idea. I'd never act on it, but I could think about it. The reality was, if I wanted him in pieces, I had six guys only too happy to do it for me. And Jackson could watch.

Nikolai approached with a tablet in his hands and nodded to Jackson. When Jackson spoke, he tapped the information into the screen, then stepped away.

"It seems to be a real place," he said.

"Good. Dispatch a team there," Yuri said. "And return our guests to their room." After a moment he added, "And supply them with some food. And coffee."

"Yes, sir," Nikolai said. He gestured for us to return back to our fancy cell.

I glanced at Jackson, reassured by his calm expression. Not even the promise of coffee was going to settle my nerves. Only getting out of here would do that.

Preferably alive and intact.

The door clicked shut behind us, only to open again ten or fifteen minutes later for George to bring in a tray of food and coffee. While Nikolai and Leopold watched, guns in hand, he placed it on the table and backed out the door. He barely gave us more than a glance.

"You think it's safe to eat?" I cast a dubious look at the plates of food and steaming mugs.

"I think if Yuri wanted us dead, we'd be dead," Jackson said. "Why bother to poison us?"

"Shits and giggles?" I suggested. "Easier cleanup?"

"We're going to have to take the risk. We don't want to come this far and die of starvation." He picked up a sandwich and bit into it. He made a face, like he wanted to spit it out.

"What is it?" Fuck, if that asshole poisoned Jackson, I was going to find a way to shove the sandwich down his throat. I didn't know how I would do it, but I would. "Are you okay?" I put a trembling hand on his arm.

He shook his head, then nodded. "There's raw onion on this sandwich. Why would someone put that on there?" He opened the bread and pulled off the rest.

I sagged with relief. "Evil people?" I suggested. Personally, I didn't mind raw onion, but I checked my sandwich for anything strange before I bit into it. It was nothing more terrifying than cheese, lettuce and tomato. It wasn't exciting, but it was filling enough. I washed it down with coffee, which was strong but surprisingly good.

I waited, but I didn't die, so that was a bonus.

"It's almost dark." I nodded toward the window.

It felt like a hundred years ago since we rowed out to the yacht, had a lovely meal and fucked out on the deck. As dates went, this was certainly unique.

Unfortunately.

With any luck, we'd get a second chance at being alone together. Although, knowing Zeke, he'd make sure we weren't as far away next time. Or he'd put a tracker in my earring like he did with my phone. And I'd let him.

"Let's get some rest," Jackson said. "It could be a long time before they confirm my father's location."

"I'm sorry you had to do that," I said regretfully. "Things could end really badly for him, couldn't they?"

"They could," Jackson agreed, his brow furrowed. "But he'd agree I made the right choice. If it was him or you, he would choose you too."

"No one should have to make that choice." I waited until he put down his coffee cup and wound my arms around him. "This is all kinds of fucked up."

"Yeah, but it was all kinds of fucked up before either of us were born." He grabbed his arms around me and pulled me to his chest. "The past had to catch up with him sooner or later. He knew that."

"What would he think when he knows you were the one who told them where to find him?" I inhaled the warm, musky scent of his body. Often, I found dangerous situations arousing, but I wasn't going to fuck him here. There was no way either of us would let our guards down that far.

"He'll understand," Jackson said. "He'll know I wouldn't have done it without good reason."

"Are you close?" I asked.

"Pretty close. He was the one who taught me how to drive a bus. He said you never know when you might need skills like that."

I looked up at him and smiled. "That skill certainly did come in handy. And it was hot too."

He smiled faintly. "If I get a chance to see him again, I'll let him know you think so. He'd think that's hilarious."

"He sounds like a good guy, except the whole torturing people for fun part. Do you think any of that is true?" It wouldn't be the first time someone made up something to falsely incriminate someone else.

"Honestly, I have no idea," Jackson admitted.

"Believe it or not, it never came up in conversation. How would I even start that anyway? 'Hey, Dad, did you torture people for the hell of it?'"

"Sometimes the direct approach is the best approach," I said. "But it's not something I would ask my father either."

His eyebrows dipped briefly. "Is there any suggestion your father was involved in anything dubious or illegal?"

I thought about that for a moment. "Seriously, once upon a time, I would have laughed at that suggestion. But now, I've come to realise people can surprise you. Maybe you never really know a person completely. Sometimes that's a bad thing and sometimes it's a good thing. If we knew everything there was to know about each other, then where would you go from there? Wouldn't things start to get boring eventually? Having some guesswork keeps things interesting. Spicy."

"Things with you will never get boring," he said firmly. "Interesting and spicy are two fantastic words to describe you. I can't imagine a day going by when you wouldn't say something or do something that takes me by surprise. And with eight of us in this relationship now, we have eight times the surprises."

"Maybe we can stick to pleasant surprises after

this," I said dryly. I'd had more than enough nasty ones for one lifetime.

"I'm all for that." He kissed my forehead, then led me over to the bed and settled us both down on top of the covers.

"Get some sleep. I'll wake you when the time is right."

I didn't think I could sleep, but when I closed my eyes I was out within a minute or two. I'd need my rest for the coming hours.

10

ABBIE

"Are you sure about this?"

Jackson blew out a breath through pursed lips, but said "I'm sure. It's the only way we're getting out of here."

"When you put it that way…" I gripped the end of his top cock piercing between the thumb and forefinger of one hand, and the ball with the other. While he carefully held his cock, I started to rotate the ball, unwinding it from the bar.

He was still as I slowly slid the bar out of his cock.

"Lucky I needed extra long bars," he said, looking smug.

Men.

"Don't make me stab you in the eyeball with this."

I wielded the bar in front of his face before I handed it to him.

"Death by cock piercing," he mused. "It would be a unique way to go."

"Don't sound so cheerful about it." I shook my head at him and followed him over to the door. The only light in the room was the moonlight. Hopefully that would be enough for him to do what he needed to do.

"When this is over, I look forward to letting you put this back." He held up the bar for a moment, then slipped it into the lock.

"I look forward to putting it back while you explain how you learnt how to pick locks," I said.

"Deal. We should probably be quiet now." His brow creased in concentration for a minute, two minutes. Finally, his teeth flashed white and he straightened up. He handed me the bar and I quickly screwed the ball back on loosely before tucking them into my pocket. Wouldn't want to lose a perfectly good cock piercing.

"Stay behind me," he whispered. He eased the door open a crack and peered out.

My heart raced like crazy. Loud enough I'd swear someone would hear it.

The door swung open silently before he crept out. He gestured behind him, for me to stay put. A moment later, a grunt was followed by a soft thud, then Jackson stuck his face back into the room.

"Come on," he hissed.

Walking silently as I could on the hardwood floor, I followed him out, almost tripping over Leopold, who was lying just outside the door.

"Is he..."

"Just out cold," Jackson said. "No idea how long he'll stay that way."

Right. If Jackson was one of the other guys, Leopold would be dead right now. Okay, maybe not Penn or Landon, but one of the others wouldn't have hesitated to kill him.

Hoping like hell I didn't wake him, I slipped the gun out of Leopold's fingers and held it loosely in my hand. I hoped I didn't have to use it. I knew how, the other guys made sure of that, but I didn't want to kill or injure anyone if I didn't have to. But if it came down to them or me, I knew which one I'd choose.

Jackson grabbed my other hand and we walked down the corridor toward the kitchen area. Yuri and the other assholes must be asleep, because the place was dark and silent. Apparently they'd underestimated our ability to use a cock piercing to escape. Their bad.

To be fair, it's not something I would have

guessed would happen either. I mean, who does shit like that? Us, apparently.

We were halfway across the room when a sound made us freeze. Jackson pulled me down behind the couch just as someone stepped into the kitchen. They opened the fridge, pulled something out and closed it again.

Okay, they wouldn't be the first person in the world to have a midnight snack. I might have done it once or twice myself.

I held my breath and waited while they ate their snack.

After what felt like a decade, they finally walked out of the kitchen and back down the corridor. The door at the end opened and then clicked shut.

I let out my breath in a silent whoosh and rose when Jackson tugged my hand.

We crept over to the door and he put his hand on the lock. The sound it made when it unlocked seemed as loud as thunder.

I winced and waited for the bad guys to come running.

No one did until we stepped out into the humid, predawn air. If I had to guess, I'd say we were three or four hours from sunrise. The only sound was the ocean lapping on the beach, and the buzz of some kind of insect.

That was, until Leopold came lumbering toward us, murmuring something incoherent. I couldn't tell if it was rage or if he wasn't speaking English.

He shouted something and raised his hand.

I acted without thinking. For all I knew, he had more than one gun or had stopped long enough to grab one. Either way, I wasn't going to wait to find out. I raised the gun and fired, getting him square in the centre of his chest.

My first thought was, *Fuck yeah, the guys would be proud of me.*

The second thought came as Leopold flew backwards and crashed to the floor. *Fuck, was he dead?*

"We need to get out of here," Jackson said urgently. "There's no way they didn't hear that." After a moment he added, "Freak out later. Come on."

I nodded and let him drag me out and away from the house. Lights blazed on inside, and assholes started shouting. They must have found Leopold already. And the open door. With any luck, they'd check our room before they looked out here. They might assume a rescue party turned up to save us and was on their way to our gilded cell.

Whatever, we couldn't assume anything so we ran, stumbling every few steps over bumps and hollows in the lawn, or stray sticks. Somehow, we managed to keep each other on our feet before we slipped into the trees a few metres from the beach.

"We need to get to the dock." He tugged me in that direction.

I glanced at the house. A couple of baddies stood out the front, silhouetted in the light. It wasn't going to take them long to figure out which way we were headed. They had the advantage of knowing this place much better than we did. We had desperation on our side, if nothing more.

We hurried toward the dock, not bothering to stay quiet. Speed was what mattered now, not stealth.

No one was at the dock when we skidded to a stop there. Two boats were tied up, the one we'd arrived on and a small rowboat.

To my surprise, it was the rowboat Jackson gestured for me to jump into.

"Wouldn't the other one be faster?" I asked.

"Faster, but louder," he said. "Stay here." He stepped up to the other bollard and started to untie the rope that tethered the bigger boat to the dock.

In about fifteen seconds flat, he had it undone and threw the rope onto the deck of the boat. He leaned to press his hands against the hull and gave it a shove. Just when I thought he would fall face first into the water, he straightened up and followed me into the rowboat.

He grabbed the oars and started to row, keeping out of the way of the other boat that was now floating free on the tide.

I was almost blinded as the dock was suddenly illuminated with floodlights. I threw a hand over my face and ducked down lower.

Lucky I did, because a bullet whizzed right over where my head just was. If I hadn't moved, I would be dead.

I won't lie, I didn't want to kill anyone, but when they shot first, then all bets were off.

I straightened enough to get off a shot, narrowly missing getting Nikolai in the leg. So much for being the reasonable kidnapper.

He aimed at me again but missed my shoulder by a hair.

"I'm starting to dislike this guy." I aimed at his groin, since I seemed to have a knack for hitting that part of the body, and got him square in his thigh.

He growled and got off another shot, this time grazing my upper arm.

Pain blossomed through my bicep and I cried out.

"Abbie? Are you all right?" Jackson's eyes were

wild with worry, but he didn't slow his rowing for more than a beat.

"I'm fine," I said quickly. It hurt like a bitch, but I'd live.

Nikolai tried again but we were too far away and the bullets only hit the water with a spray, before they sank uselessly to the bottom of the ocean.

I snorted a laugh, but only a small one. We weren't safe yet. I wouldn't relax until we were.

"You're a badass," Jackson said approvingly. "Are you sure you're okay?"

"It's just a graze," I said. "Don't dudes dig chicks with scars?" If they didn't, then they should. Especially since I got this one helping to save our asses.

"I dig you, with or without scars," he said. "But I prefer you alive and unhurt."

"You too," I said. And me too. I much preferred myself alive and unhurt.

I looked back at the house. All of the baddies, including Yuri, were gathered on the dock. If I had to guess, I'd think they were trying to figure out how to get the other boat back so they could come after us. Someone was going to have to swim out to it and that would take time. Time for us to get the fuck out of here.

"It's going to be a long way back to the island this way," I said. "Do you want me to take a turn rowing?"

I pressed a couple of fingers to my wound to stop it from bleeding. Rowing would hurt like a bitch too, but I'd do it if he needed a break.

"I'm good," he said. "We won't need to row all the way back, unless I'm wrong."

"Wrong about what?" I frowned at him.

"Wrong about how Yuri got here." He jerked his head behind him, toward a dark shape that bobbed on the swell. I hadn't noticed it until now, but it grew bigger and bigger by the moment.

"Another yacht?" The question was rhetorical. What else would be floating around out here? It certainly wasn't a huge, inflatable unicorn. It wasn't even a huge, inflatable penis. That sucked, because one of those would be fun. Okay, maybe not out here in the middle of the ocean, in the dark. Another time maybe.

We slid across the water towards it, silent except for the dip of the oars every couple of seconds. When we were about twenty metres out, I saw how big the yacht really was. Superyacht might be a better name for it. Low lights glittered here or there, for the convenience of the crew. If anyone stood watch, I couldn't see them. Presumably Yuri thought his little toy was safe out here.

"Do you know how to drive a yacht?" Was drive the right word? Whatever, he knew what I meant.

"Everything is operated with computers these days," he said. "How hard can it be?"

"That would be no then," I concluded. He was right though, how hard *could* it be? The bigger problem might be dealing with the crew, who could very well be innocent.

About ten metres from the superyacht, another sound echoed across the water.

"Shit," Jackson said softly.

I looked back the way we came to see the lights of the other boat, Yuri and the other kidnappers on board. They headed towards us with all the speed of a vessel with an actual engine. As fast as Jackson was, he couldn't out-row a motorboat. And now we were stuck between that and the yacht.

"Shit is right," I said softly.

11

ABBIE

"Grab the ladder," Jackson said. "We need to get on board before they get close enough to shoot."

I grabbed the closest rung and pulled, until the side of the rowboat bumped against the yacht. Climbing with a gun in one hand wasn't the easiest thing I've ever done, but I wasn't going to let it go. I sure as hell wasn't going to put it in my pocket and risk shooting myself in the foot. With my luck, that would be exactly what happened.

I pulled myself over onto the deck and dropped down lightly. I turned back to the railing as Jackson grabbed the ladder.

They were almost in range.

George raised his gun and peppered the other side of the rowboat with bullets. It quickly started to take on water, but Jackson was clear by then.

"Come on," I urged him. "You're nearly there."

Another shot rang out and Jackson grunted.

"Jax!" I called out frantically. "Come on, babe."

His breathing was laboured. He was obviously winded from the effort of rowing, and in pain, but he kept on climbing.

George aimed again, but I pointed my gun at him and squeezed the trigger. George ducked and the shot missed him, but hit Nikolai in the stomach. He went down like a bag of potatoes.

"Give it up," Yuri shouted over the water. "You have nowhere to go. I know you're both injured. Surrender now and you might get to live."

As offers went, that was pretty crappy. Why would I surrender when all he could give me was a maybe?

Jackson reached the top of the ladder and I leaned down to help him up. "Where did he get you?"

"In my ass," he said with another grunt of pain, mixed with one of frustration and a sprinkle of humiliation.

I frowned. "Bummer."

He gave me a faint smile. "Yeah, just a bit. At least he didn't shoot me in the cock."

"He wouldn't dare," I growled. I helped him over the railing and down to the deck. "Maybe we should take a leaf from their book."

I ducked down low and peered over the railing. The rowboat was already half full of water. No one was using that ever again.

I raised the gun and aimed at the hull of the other boat. My aim was off. I missed the hull and hit the engine instead.

Unfortunately, it didn't burst into flames like it would in the movies, but it did sputter and die.

"Looks like someone's going to have to get out and swim," I remarked.

"Sucks to be them." Jackson was looking around like he might actually be able to see his own ass. Blood already coated the back of his pants and seeped down his leg.

"We need to get you to a doctor," I said. Me too, because I was also covered in blood. "Preferably before anyone tries to stop us." Voices sounded from inside the yacht and a couple of lights flickered on.

"Are we going to be able to steal this thing?"

"I have a better idea," Jackson said. "Come on."

"Please tell me it's not another rowboat," I said.

He grinned and let me around to the back deck of the yacht. Was this the poop deck? What even was a poop deck? I didn't know, I'd look up later. After I dealt with what I was staring at.

I blinked.

"Are you out of your mind?"

"You have a better idea?" he asked.

"No, but do you know how to fly one of those?" Had he hit his head at some point, or was he even more of a badass than I thought?

"My father also thought flying a helicopter would be a useful skill I might need some day." He ushered me towards it and opened the door. "In you get."

He closed the door behind me and trotted around to the other side. He winced as he slipped into the seat and clicked in his seatbelt.

"Normally I'd do a pre-flight safety check, but we don't have time for that." He pressed the button to turn on the helicopter's engine and the rotors started to turn.

"This isn't going to go unnoticed." I slipped on the set of headphones he handed me before he put on his own.

"Probably not," he agreed. "Keep your eyes open."

I took that to mean, 'be ready to shoot anyone who comes along and tries to stop us.' I had no idea how many bullets I had left, if I even had any, but I could wave it around and potentially deter people.

The rotors were turning faster now, just a blur out the window, barely visible in the early light of the morning.

With a jolt, the helicopter lifted up off the yacht's helipad and into the sky.

I held my breath. We were a very clear, very obvious target right now. A target for assholes who probably knew where to aim to make the helicopter explode or crash back down to the deck.

Goody.

Jackson banked the helicopter slightly and flew in the opposite direction of Yuri and George. By now, several people appeared from below decks and watched us take off.

We quickly rose to a height beyond the range of a handgun, and Jackson took us in a wide circle around the superyacht.

I spotted George in the water, pulling a rope behind him, towing Yuri and the smaller boat to the yacht.

"Who says it's hard to get good help these days?" I asked.

Jackson laughed. "It's funny the things people do if you pay them enough."

"That's true. You definitely deserve a pay raise after this. Maybe Levi will let you keep the helicopter."

"Then I'd spend half my life taking Asher on joy rides around whatever city we're in." He pressed a couple of buttons, the use of which I could only guess at.

"That doesn't sound so bad." I waved at Yuri as we

passed overhead. He might have waved back and he might have been flipping me off.

Sorry not sorry, asshole.

"Yeah, but he'd want to fuck in the back seat, instead of enjoying the flight." Jackson looked over at me and smiled a panty melting smile.

"Is it wrong that this is really, really hot?" I said. "I mean, we're both injured, we got kidnapped at gunpoint and shot at. I shot a couple of people and all I can think is how sexy it is that you can fly a helicopter."

"Priorities," he said with a firm nod. "It should also bear in mind that IslandFest starts in a few hours. If we're lucky, we'll get you back there in time."

I swore under my breath. "I forgot all about it. I was kind of busy trying not to die." If I didn't turn up, something else would die—my career. I hadn't worked my cute little butt off to throw it away now. Or have it taken away from me by asshole kidnappers.

"What's going to happen to your father?" I asked.

"The location I gave them was an old one," he said. "He and my mother are long gone from there. It'll look like he just left, but they won't find him." He pressed a couple of different buttons and switches.

"It was never going to be that easy to find him. He's like a fox."

"But they'll keep looking?" I guessed.

He looked over quickly and nodded, before turning back to the controls. "Yes, they'll keep on looking. They'll look until they find him or he dies of old age. Whichever happens first."

"And they're not going to stop asking you where he is, will they? Yuri is going to keep on coming."

"Yuri will go underground after this," Jackson said. "Someone else might pop up, but I'll make it known that I don't know where he is. At this moment, I really don't. It's safer for him and me if it stays that way." His denim blue eyes looked sad at the idea of never seeing his father again. Or his mother, for that matter.

"I'm sorry about that," I said sincerely. I couldn't begin to understand how that would feel. Knowing they were out there somewhere and never knowing where that was. Always wondering if they might turn up alive or otherwise.

He shrugged one shoulder. "I have another family now anyway. You and all the boys. And Levi is like another brother to me." He hesitated for a moment, then said, "Both of my families have almost gotten me killed in the last few months."

"Several times," I agreed. "What is family for if they can't put you in danger from time to time?"

He chuckled. "They're pretty good at getting me out of danger as well, so there's that."

"At least life is interesting." A little peace and quiet might be nice for a while. But it was kinda cool to be in a helicopter, flying over the Caribbean.

"It certainly is." Jackson shifted in his seat. He was clearly in a lot of pain and if I had to guess, I'd say it was getting worse. That was understandable, since he was probably sitting on a bullet. That probably hurt like a motherfucker. It just went to show how much of a badass he was, that he didn't complain. He just got on with the job of flying the helicopter like some kind of action hero.

"You know, they should make a movie out of this." I kept a close eye on him, although what the fuck I'd do if he passed out, I have no idea. The best thing I could do right now was keep him talking and alert.

"Hemsworth can play me," he said immediately. "They'll have to find someone smoking hot enough to play you."

"I'm sure there are lots of actors who could play me." Maybe that blond one who won an Academy Award that time. What was her name? I couldn't remember.

"Asher is going to be really disappointed he missed all the excitement," I added. Zeke was going to be pissed. He always was when someone kidnapped me, and he didn't have family ties to Yuri to keep him from ripping the guy's head off. He'd just go ahead and do it. Tully too. Penn would give Yuri a piece of his mind first.

What would Landon and Channing do? Whatever it was, it wouldn't be pretty.

"We can act it out for him," Jackson said. "Although, he'll probably take one look at the helicopter and forget all about what he might have missed out on."

"That sounds accurate." I realised I still held the gun in my hand. "Should I get rid of this?" The last thing I needed was to have it used as evidence against me. Even if everything I did was in self-defence.

"Absolutely," Jackson agreed. "Jettison that bitch."

I carefully opened the tiny window beside me and slipped the gun through the crack. I opened my fingers and let it slide away into the air. I didn't see it land or be swallowed by the waves, but no one would find it out here.

"We should reach the island in half an hour or so," Jackson said. "Luckily the bad guys stocked the chopper with enough fuel." He pressed a button in front of me and talked into his headphones.

"This is the island airport," a voice came through both of our headphones. "I see your approach. I'll clear you for landing."

I realised that, as hot as seeing Jackson fly a helicopter was, I was looking forward to having my feet back on solid ground and the other guys' arms around us both.

12

ZEKE

I curled and uncurled my hands to keep from punching something. Or some*one*.

"Absolutely, fucking nothing," I growled. "It's like they disappeared off the face of the planet. I don't think the authorities believe me when I say they weren't on that yacht."

Levi nodded, his expression grim. "It's been how long? About thirty hours?"

"Too fucking long." I stalked from one side of the room to the other. "I've had everyone I know looking into this Yuri guy, but so far nothing on him either. You said he was after Jackson's father?"

I should have known Jackson was into some shady shit. The rest of us were, and he rolled with it. Whether it was being ambushed or having to dispose of disembodied heads, he dealt with it. It never occurred to me to question why.

Levi sipped his coffee and looked way too cool under the circumstances. "He didn't tell me much, but that was about the gist of it. He's dropped by Jackson's house a time or two, but I don't think he expected it to escalate."

I rubbed a hand over the back of my head. "I wish he'd come to me. I might have been able to do something to prevent it." If this guy was the one behind Abbie and Jackson's disappearance. There were still some dubious players in the game, like the Bell family, but this didn't feel like any of them. They would have waited until we were all together and taken us all out. And, as far as I knew, the Bells had no argument with Abbie or Jackson. Unless...

I shook my head to myself. There were too many ifs and buts, and right now it didn't matter who did this, as long as we got them back.

"You can't fucking babysit all of us all the time," Penn snapped. He gave me a look like he thought I was overreacting, but he was as worried as the rest of us. I saw it on his face and in every agitated movement. More agitated than usual.

"Can't I?" I retorted. "I don't remember you objecting when I saved your ass a couple of times."

Before Penn could respond, Asher stepped in

between us and slipped his arms around my neck. "Fighting with each other isn't going to get us anywhere. We need to support each other right now. We're all worried about them. We would all do anything to get them back."

I closed my eyes and pressed my cheek to his. Neither of us had shaved for a couple of days and our stubble clashed and scratched, but I drew strength from his touch.

"I wish I knew what we had to do, that's all," I said. "Who do we have to kill to get them back to us? Point me in the right direction and I'll go."

"And we'll go with you," Landon said. "Right, Channing?"

"Without doubt," Channing agreed. "We all feel as helpless as you do."

I looked over at him and wanted to dispute that, but I couldn't. The expression on his face, on all of their faces, were a match for mine.

"I don't suppose the label got a ransom note?" Tully asked. He looked very sure the answer would be no. And it was.

Levi shook his head. "No, which is just as well because I don't think the label has enough money to pay what either of them are worth." He sighed heavily. "No, I might not have the background you guys do, but thinking back at the way Jackson talked about Yuri, it makes sense that he or someone like him was behind this."

Which brought me back to wishing Jackson confided in me. I would never have let him and Abbie go on that yacht if I'd known there was this kind of risk out there. Which was exactly why he didn't tell me. Like Penn so eloquently said, I couldn't babysit them all the time.

"The ocean is a big place," Asher said. "It will take a bunch of boats to cover it."

"A fleet," Penn said. When we all turned to look at him he said, "A bunch of boats is called a *fleet.*"

Asher shrugged, his chest rising and falling against mine. "Whatever."

Penn muttered something about accuracy, but otherwise fell quiet.

Asher shook his head. "What was I saying?"

"Well if you don't know, babe…" I teased lightly. I kissed his mouth before he could retort, then pulled back. "What were you saying? Something about a bunch of boats." I shot Penn a warning look before he commented.

"Right." Asher frowned adorably. "Maybe we need something better than a bunch of boats. Like a plane. Or—"

"A helicopter," Landon said.

Asher snapped his fingers and flicked a finger gun at Landon. "Exactly. A helicopter."

"No," Landon said. "I hear a helicopter. Maybe they know something."

I listened. He was right, there was a helicopter headed towards the island. If I had to guess, I'd say it was coming in fast and low.

"The airport is on the other side of the island." Tully frowned.

I nodded and headed out the door without another word, my fingers curled around Asher's.

We trotted out to the field where the organisers were still setting up for the festival. A stage sat along on one end, wide enough and deep enough for even the biggest bands. Speakers were arrayed around it, big enough that the music would be heard on the other side of the island.

The centre of the field was open, but ringed with portable toilets and other amenities. Right now, it was also full of people. Many lay around on blankets or towels, claiming the best vantage point for themselves.

On the other side of the amenities was a sea of tents. This was usually were one of the guys would have mentioned how much fucking would go on inside, and outside, those tents. Not today though. Today, we stood with our hands shielding our eyes, watching the helicopter approach.

I was right, it was coming in fast, and wobbling now and then, like it was either on the breeze or the pilot couldn't keep it straight.

"Um…" Asher said.

"Right," I said. I put my hands around my mouth and shouted, "Clear the field!"

For a solid thirty seconds I thought everyone was going to ignore me. Then they noticed the big ass fuck helicopter headed straight for the field and scattered like scared sheep. Several tripped and almost fell, but managed to get out of the way right before the helicopter bumped down onto the grass.

It rose again, did a half-turn and then came to rest before the engine died.

"What the fuck?" Penn muttered.

For once, I agreed with him. I hurried towards the helicopter, eyes wary, expecting trouble.

I didn't expect the passenger door to pop open and Abbie to slip out. She kept her head down, away from the still turning rotors and hurried around to the other side of the helicopter.

"He's injured," she said, her voice and eyes as wild as her hair.

"So are you." One of her sleeves was covered in blood.

She glanced at it as though she'd forgotten all about it. "It's nothing. We need to get Jackson to hospital." She put a hand on the pilot's side door and yanked it open.

Jackson looked pale. He was also covered in blood, but he was alive. He even managed to say, "Hey, it's good to see you," before he almost tumbled out of the helicopter.

I managed to grab him and with Asher and Abbie's help, stop him from falling onto the grass. The pilot's seat was covered in blood. Not enough to kill him, but enough that he was going to be out of it for a day or two.

The other guys, without having to be told, arrayed themselves around Abbie and Jackson to shield them from the people gawking. That didn't stop people from trying to look, or taking photos. No doubt there were at least a dozen videos of the helicopter landing and Abbie getting out being uploaded to the Internet as we spoke.

"There's a medical tent over here," Levi said, waving a few metres away.

"Can you walk?" I hooked one of Jackson's arms over my shoulder and, to my surprise, Penn did the same on the other side.

"I'm all right," Jackson protested.

"He got shot in the ass and hasn't slept since we got taken," Abbie said.

"Yeah, all I need is some sleep," Jackson agreed.

"You're in the wrong place for that." Penn snorted. "No one is going to be sleeping around here for a couple of days."

Jackson gave him a sidelong look. "Thanks. Love you too."

Penn shrugged his other shoulder. "Didn't say I don't love you, just saying—"

"We get it," I said.

We helped Jackson into the medical tent and down onto one of the low camp beds. While a nurse tended to his ass, I finally got a chance to turn to Abbie. I pulled into my arms and kissed her, long and deep.

Then I pulled back and said, "Where the hell were you? We've been going crazy trying to figure out how to find you."

"Out and about," she said lightly. "Would you believe we went for a joyride?"

I raised my eyebrows at her. "I fucking hope not, because most joyrides don't end up in blood, or with landing a helicopter in the middle of a field of people."

"Jackson was going to land at the airport but he

was getting faint," she explained. "It was that or ditch in the ocean."

"I'm glad he chose that." Later, he was going to have to tell me how the hell he knew how to fly a helicopter. I kissed her again before I was all but shoved aside so Asher could kiss her. Then Tully. Then Penn. Then Landon and Channing together.

Levi even managed to give her a hug. "If you wanted to generate some extra publicity, you could have asked." He grinned.

"I thought I'd surprise you," she said sarcastically. "What do you think?"

"Best fucking entrance ever," Asher said. "I think we should arrive that way for all of our concerts from now on. Minus the injuries."

"Asher is paying for the use of the helicopter," Penn said dryly.

"I'm actually tempted," Asher said. "Just because it would be that awesome."

"You're an idiot," Penn told him.

"Love you too," Asher told him.

Penn rolled his eyes in response.

"Excuse me, but your manager will be fine," the nurse said. "Nothing I couldn't fix up myself and he only needed a handful of stitches." She looked like she pulled bullets out of asses often enough that she didn't even think twice about them anymore. Maybe she did. I bet nurses saw all kinds of things on a daily basis, so nothing much was new anymore.

"He's going to need something for the pain the next day or so, but otherwise I recommend rest. As much of it as he will get here anyway." She nodded and walked away to tend to somebody else.

"He's lucky," I said slowly. "This way, I can't kick him in the ass."

Abbie placed her hands on her hips. "None of this was his fault. If it wasn't for him, we'd still be there. Or dead."

"If it wasn't for Abbie, we'd be dead," Jackson said, stepping towards us, a pained expression on his face. "Be careful around her when she has a gun in her hand." He added that last bit low, so no one else could hear.

"Sounds like we missed all the fun." Asher looked rueful.

Abbie put her arm around him and rested her head against his chest. "Trust me, you didn't miss a thing. And we didn't miss IslandFest. But what I need right now is a long, hot shower."

We stepped out of the medical tent to a loud round of cheers from the concertgoers gathered there. Most of them had their phones up, filming us. Specifically, filming Abbie.

"That was fucking epic!" someone shouted.

Someone else started to chant and one by one everyone took it up. "Abbie! Abbie! Abbie!"

"Oi! Oi! Oi!" Asher shouted in reply.

The crowd laughed and changed the chant to, "Venom! Venom! Venom!"

"No one knows how to please a crowd like Wolf Venom and Abbie." Levi grinned.

"We're definitely a hard act to follow," I agreed. "But you know what, I'm sure the band after us will be just as awesome."

To the shouts of the crowd, we headed back to our hotel rooms. We had some unfinished business to attend to.

13

ABBIE

"Best festival ever," Asher declared.

We walked back to our hotel room after the last band of the festival finished. The exhausted, but still hyped, crowds cheered almost as loud as they'd played.

"It really fucking was," Landon agreed. "I hope they invite us back next time."

"I hope next time I don't go viral for arriving in a helicopter." I glanced over at Jackson and smiled. He was still walking a little stiffly, but a lot more easily than a couple of days ago.

The guys hadn't let the poor guy sleep until they heard every detail of our kidnapping and escape. According to Zeke, Yuri was long gone before any authorities arrived. As we suspected, the house didn't belong to him. Neither did the superyacht. If anyone else was involved, no one had any answers.

"Do you know how many bands have approached me to be their manager?" Jackson asked.

"Is it zero?" Penn cocked an eyebrow at him.

Jackson pretended to look insulted. "No, it wasn't zero. There were three, but they were very insistent."

"You told them no though, right?" Zeke asked. "I hope so, because I'd hate to have to hurt anyone."

"You're stuck with me," Jackson said. "If only to keep people safe from you." He gave Zeke a faint but affectionate smile.

"Whatever it takes, bro." Zeke slapped him on the back.

"You guys are all idiots," Penn said.

"Yeah, but you're all my idiots," I said, including him in the insult.

"I knew there was a reason I still hate you." But the look Penn gave me was loving and, for him, soft.

"I hate you too." I returned his look.

Moving so quickly he made me squeal, he scooped me up in his arms and carried me into the hotel. He lay me down on the bed and lay over me. Before he kissed me he said, "If anyone else wants in on this, we don't mind."

He claimed my mouth in a searing kiss that made

me forget everything, and slid his hands up under my top.

"We're in," Asher said. He grabbed the hem of his shirt and tugged it up over his head with one hand, then reached for Zeke and dragged him down beside us.

The bed dipped on the other side and I expected to see Tully, but it was Jackson who lay down next to us. He looked nervous. That wasn't surprising. His experience of us fucking as a group, was walking in on us one time in one of the stadiums. He gave me a lecture about closing the door. I'd always suspected he'd wanted to join in.

"Are you sure?" I asked softly.

"I am if you guys are," he said carefully. This would change his relationship with the other guys forever. I think on some level we all knew that. Hopefully it would be for the better.

"The more, the merrier," Tully said. He sat near the end of the bed and started to pull off my skirt and panties.

Between Penn and Jackson, they helped me out of my shirt and bra, then stripped off their clothes.

I heard the sound of scraping and picked up my head to see Landon and Channing push the other bed over so we had one long bed. Then they were also naked.

Everywhere I looked, there was a naked hot guy. Not just that, but naked hot guys who loved me. Whom I loved. Lucky me.

I lay back and Penn kissed me while Jackson ran his hands around and over my breasts, touching and feeling like he wanted to memorise every centimetre.

Tully gently parted my thighs with his hands and lowered his face between my legs. He circled my clit with his tongue, teasing and tasting, but not quite touching.

"Please," I groaned. "I need…"

"We know what you need," Penn said. "Let's not rush it." Before I could glare, or retort, he slanted his mouth over mine and kissed me, cutting off words before they were formed. He thrust his tongue between my lips like he was fucking my mouth with it.

I sucked eagerly, like it was his cock.

The warmth of Jackson's mouth clamped lightly over one of my nipples. He grazed my sensitive, pebbled peak with his teeth.

Tully chose a moment to slip one, two of his long fingers inside me and draw my clit in between his lips.

I shivered with delight. My whole body was on fire with all the sensations all at once. Every one of my senses were stimulated almost to the point of overload. The taste of Penn, the feel of Tully and Jackson, the smell of desire, the sight of Penn's bright blue eyes so close to mine, the sound of sucking and licking and kissing.

Every single one of us was a part of this.

It was divine.

Penn loved to tell me when I could come and when I couldn't, but there was no way he could have stopped me, nothing he could have said. The orgasm pounded through me louder than any of the bands at IslandFest, harder than the hardest rock song. I shattered into a million little pieces and cried out against Penn's mouth.

Tully didn't stop working me, teasing until I came back down and flopped against the mattress. Only then, he pulled away his face and slid his fingers out of me.

Penn leaned looked at me like I shouldn't have come without his say so, but he said, "My turn."

He swapped places with Tully, the lead guitarist coming to lie beside me. He kissed me, tasting my juices. "You're so delicious."

"I could say the same about you." There was something about a guy who tasted of my orgasm. Especially when he was the one who made me come.

"You're so fucking wet," Penn said. "I'm starting to think fucking is your favourite thing."

I gave him a husky laugh in response. "It definitely is. That and music. And you guys."

"I'm glad you added that last bit." He wasn't gentle when he thrust three fingers into me, not even a little bit. He worked me hard with his hand and mouth, like he was determined to push me to the edge as quickly as possible.

That was exactly what he did, but before I tipped over, he took his hand away and kissed up and down the insides of my thighs.

At the same time, Tully and Jackson took turns lavishing attention on my breasts and kissing my mouth. I felt like the centre of the universe. Or at least, their universe.

Just before I went completely crazy, Penn started to work me again, harder this time; relentless.

"Good girl, come, right now," he ordered.

Whether it was his words, his actions or a combination, I did exactly that. I arched my back and dug my nails into Jackson's arm. I closed my eyes and pressed my lips together. I rocked my body so hard I didn't know how my spine didn't snap. I cried out so loud most of the island probably heard me.

I finally flopped down and lay panting, letting the blood return to the rest of my body.

"Good girl," Penn said again. "Now you're all witnesses to the fact she can do as she's told once in a while." He looked smug.

I snorted breathlessly and said, "Fuck off."

He just grinned. "Jackson's turn."

Jackson looked like he wasn't sure if he was going to do it Penn told him to do, but apparently making me come again was worth being bossed around for.

I wasn't sure I *could* come a third time, but the sight of Asher with his mouth around Zeke's cock, Zeke's fingers tangled in his hair, and Landon and Channing lying head to feet with each other's cocks in their mouths drove me to the edge a third and then a fourth time.

Apparently it had the same effect on Zeke, because he came too. "Fuck, fuck, fuck. Yeah."

Penn scooted up next to me. "Open up, you dirty bitch." He liked to mix up his praise with his dirty talk. He tapped my lips with his cock.

I gave him a look like I might disobey, but then opened to let him slip his cock into my mouth.

Jackson, mouth shining, eyes on me, knelt between my thighs and carefully slid his cock into my body.

Someone, I don't know who, handed around a tube of lube. The guys rolled me over so I straddled Jackson.

"Lean forward," Penn ordered.

Jackson raised his eyebrows. I smiled reassuringly at him. He knew if he wanted us to stop, he only had to say so. We were all about consent and respect.

I leaned over Jackson while Tully lubricated my rear hole. His finger was cold, making me shiver before I took a deep breath and relaxed, appreciating the way he opened me up, readied me for him.

He tossed the lube to someone else, placed his hands on my hips and slowly slid himself inside.

On one side of me, Channing did the same to Landon, while on the other Asher did the same to Zeke.

Holy shit.

I managed a glance at Jackson's face at the point where Tully's cock must have touched his. His eyes widened, but then half closed again. Yeah, this might change everything for all of us, but it was definitely a change for the better. Jackson was very much one of us now.

All around me, and inside me were the slow steady thrusts and pants of seven guys. The whole world was gone and everything left was this moment and all eight of us.

One by one, the guys came, a series of grunts and moans and the occasional, "Fuck yeah."

I came again, right at the point when Jackson and Tully both did. They both stilled inside me, only a narrow wall of my body between their cocks. They were so close, they must have felt each other's rush of warmth, the squirt of pearly cum into me. That might be the hottest thing yet. It was followed closely by Penn slamming between my lips and spilling his salty release into my mouth. I waited until he pulled out before locking my eyes on his and swallowing down every drop.

"Good girl. You're not so bad after all."

I slapped Penn on the chest with the back of my hand, but it was a half-hearted effort at best. "Neither are you," I said. "Mostly."

He chuckled and lay next to me, his hand on my hip.

Tully and Jackson lay on the other side, with all the other guys spread out around us.

We all sagged together in a heap of arms and legs and satisfaction. We snuggled down together and finally slept.

One big crazy, blissed out family.

THANK FOR READING! If you loved this novella, please leave a review

For more dark mafia hotness, the next stop is Bait. Dark Masque book 1!

ABOUT THE AUTHOR

Maggie Alabaster writes reverse harem and, paranormal, sci-fi and fantasy romance.

She lives in NSW, Australia with one spouse, two daughters, one dog, and countless birds.

Jo Bradley writes contemporary romance.

Sign up for Maggie's newsletter! Sign Up!

Join Maggie's reader group! Join here!

Follow Maggie on Bookbub! Click here to follow me!

Check out Maggie's website- www.maggiealabaster.com

Sign up for Jo's newsletter

Book 3 Pursued by Monsters